I0593345

Joined
in Fire

The Altered Elite Series
Book 2

D. Burgard

Joined in Fire

Paperback ISBN: 978-0-9857582-5-7
Ebook ISBN: 978-0-9857582-4-0

Contents

For the Burgard Boys,
one thru four

The Altered Elite Series

—

The Amber Torch
Book 1

Joined in Fire
Book 2

The Imminent Storm
Book 3

Book 4 coming soon!

dburgardbooks.com

Joined
in Fire

1

—

Running, I'm reactive as the mountain looming ahead beckons. I can feel my body transitioning even as the yearning threatens to overwhelm my senses. The rage I felt just a few minutes ago is already fading with every step I take. So much so that it won't be long before all I'm left with is the all-encompassing need that makes my body ache to run.

With everything that's happened, I can't help but hate this thing, concealed up in the mountain, summoning me like its slave. For keeping me distracted, diverted from taking even a small moment to wrap my head around my fury. So many people have been hurt, but I don't get a moment—not even one moment—to digest it.

The terrain is changing rapidly. The ground is becoming softer, more giving with every step. I can see flashes of green and feel a slight twinge of moisture in the air. My lungs, so parched, suck in every drop. I'm able to use a little of that moisture to swipe my tongue over the deep cracks in my lips, but I'm left with a repulsive copper taste in my mouth. Another reminder of what I've been through.

My mind, a blur of images, can't distract me as I respond to the pull. I can only assume I'm going through the final stages of this change, and I have no choice but to keep running toward the one thing that will complete my transformation.

Getting closer, I'm feeling tired, exhausted even, but I'm strangely comforted nonetheless by my closeness to the mountain.

The need in me wanes slightly as my pace slows. I'm able to regain some semblance of my senses as I look around at the forest that surrounds me. The spruce and fir trees are abundant. My body seems to know the route, even if I don't consciously remember it.

To those lucky enough to have it, being normal can seem boring. Most of the time, it's taken for granted and sometimes it's even wished away. Some people want to be extraordinary.

I know how cruel and horrible being extraordinary can be. Fists clenched, I feel my body respond as my thoughts rage within me. I struggle to keep my emotions in check, but it's no use, I'm too far gone. I fall to my knees gasping as a sharp pain slices through my abdomen. I can't move and don't dare breathe. My eyes dart to the glow coming from my chest, illuminating my shirt in the places not soaked through with blood.

What will I become when this transformation is complete?

The pain begins to subside. I feel my heart rate slow as the light under my shirt fades. Standing, I'm instantly reminded of my body's intentions as the yearning begins again.

Unable to gain control as my body quickly transitions, I take off running. That word jumps in my head again—extraordinary. I sprint along for another minute until something alters my awareness.

I stop and crouch down. Peering over a huge rock, I'm able to see some fifty yards or so ahead. What draws my attention isn't just the number of persons, dressed in similar garb to their surroundings, dispersed throughout the area or the multitude of sounds that my hearing is now indescribably able to hone in on, but the opening to a cave: a cave that holds the one thing I've come to want more than I can even understand.

The cave is surrounded by armed guards. I rest my back

against the boulder and consider my next move. The way my body is reacting, I know why these men are here. Resting somewhere inside that cave is the energy source, the true source of our abilities. There are others like me.

There are people born with something unusual in their DNA. When these people start experiencing hormonal fluctuations or surges in adolescence they ... change. I don't mean change like a normal teenager during puberty. No, this is different.

These men are here to protect the source. Most likely they're protecting it from me. I feel it beckon to me again ... the extraterrestrial energy that supplies our powers, without which who knows what would happen. Most of my kind believe we would all perish. Honestly, after everything that's happened, I really don't care. Either way it goes for me, it's going to be painful. I'm sure of it.

Taking deep breaths, I try to close my eyes but am unable to. My emotions flood my mind with images that threaten to send me back into a state of chaos. I breathe slowly, trying to concentrate on the noises around me. I just sit and try to steady myself, my whole body throbbing. I need to get inside that cave.

Twigs snap, and I realize someone is running in my direction. Still leaning against the boulder, my body tenses.

"Sir, cameras four and five picked up movement," a man says out of breath.

"Was the silent alarm tripped?"

"No sir, it could have been another animal."

"Yeah, well send team three to do a perimeter sweep. If it's one of those damn snakes again, I'm gonna blow its head off."

"Yes, sir."

"Oh and Jackson, go relieve Miller. I need him here

when the call comes in."

"Yes, sir. Uh ... sir?"

"What?"

"Well sir, a couple of the men, they were wondering about the cave, I mean ... uh ...it's just, after what happened to Henry..."

I hear a sigh and there's a long pause before the man speaks, a slight edge to his voice. "You have your orders Jackson, so I'd advise you to do what I said and go relieve Miller."

"Sir."

As I hear what I can only assume is Jackson briskly walking away, dread washes over me. Whatever is in that cave has them spooked.

I smell a cigarette. One of the men must have lit one. It's out before I can stop it ... my body's protest to its slight oxygen deprivation ... a small cough.

He's beside me faster than I would have expected. With a gun pointed at my head, he commands, "Get up!"

Rising slowly, I rack my brain trying to figure a way out of this unexpected turn of events. I'm not able to think fast enough but it doesn't matter ... my body reacts anyway, and a second later the man is lying at my feet.

I fight the urge to bolt. Just then, a man's voice blares beside me. It's coming from a radio hooked to the belt of the man with the gun.

"Sir, the call from Mitchell is coming in."

There's a pause before the radio blares again. "Sir?"

Recognizing that at any moment I will no longer be alone, I peer up over the rock and see two men headed my way. They see me and break into a run.

My foot makes contact with something, and I look down to see the same black handgun that just moments before had been pointed at me. I grab it, spring up, and come face to face with one of the men, who's pointing his own weapon at me.

"You think you gonna shoot me," he snickers.

I'm taken aback by his weird reaction to having a gun pointed at him until he goes on to say, "The safety's still on."

I know what the safety on a gun does, in theory, but since I've never been around them, much less shot one before, I have no idea what to do to rectify the situation. Hearing a bullet whizzing my way from behind I quickly improvise and toss it at him. It distracts him for just a second, but a second is all I need. He gasps as I grab him and turn him into it. He grunts and crumples to the ground.

Stepping to the side the next bullet flies by. How am I able to hear them? To hone in on that distinctive click as another one is sent off on its course?

When I look over, I see two more men headed in my direction. Distracted, I hear more bullets but react too slowly.

Pain shoots through my shoulder as I cry out. Instinctively I reach out to touch its origin and feel the wetness. Blood begins to run down my arm as I dive behind a large tree next to the cave entrance. The men pound after me.

I want more than anything to just sprint for the opening to the cave but the pain gives me pause. How many more bullets can my body withstand?

Even so, my options are limited, and so I take off, expecting to feel the sting of more bullets entering my body at any second. And so I do.

Bullets bite into my back and right leg as I dive into the cool darkness.

"She's in the cave!" I hear one of the guards say in disbelief.

"No shit Jackson! Now come on."

"Wait! I ain't going in there. What about what happened to Henry?"

"Obviously, numb-nuts, the thing is turned off. If she does something to whatever's in there it's our asses. I'm not going down because I was too afraid to take some girl out!"

Every move I make is agony, but I push on, my broken body crawling ever so slowly as I hear his footsteps drawing closer. They stop and my eyes dart toward the opening of the cave. Hidden in the darkness, I'm able to watch as the guard peers in. He seems conflicted as he hesitates at the entrance, uncertainty on his face. For a brief moment, I hope that maybe he'll just turn around and walk away, but today, luck doesn't seem to be on my side.

Raising his gun, he enters the cave. Every step he takes seems deliberate and controlled. I can tell nothing is going to get by him, and in a few steps he'll step on me if he doesn't see me first.

The other two guards position themselves at the cave entrance. More cautious than the first guy, they just stand there, poised and ready but not willing to devote as much to the cause.

The bullet holes in my body ache. Images of loved ones I've lost keep finding their way into my consciousness.

Although one part of me would be happy to end all this suffering, it's that other part, the part that's changing, that has other plans.

It's the glow that catches my eyes first. The soft amber hued illumination that I've grown so accustomed to seeing at usually the most inopportune times. This time it's different. Different in the fact that it isn't coming from me but radiating from deep within the cave. My pain eases for a moment.

The guard is staring in the direction of the glowing light, too, seemingly frozen. The other two also see it. They seem spellbound, as it gets brighter by the second. That's when I realize it's not their fear that's keeping them rooted to their spot. It's the fact that they're already dead. Smoldering corpses still standing as a fire burns within.

I watch in revulsion as they fall to the ground, their faces horror-stricken along with the horrible smell of their burning flash.

The glow draws me toward it, invites me closer. I sit up easily now. The pain I felt just moments ago is completely gone. Reaching up, I pull my shirt off my shoulder to get a look at the area where the first bullet pierced my skin. There's nothing there other than crusting dried blood. No entry wound, not even a scratch. I'm healed.

As the light gets brighter, I'm able to see the inside of the cave more clearly. It's not a big cave, but there seems to be a large recess in the back from where the light is coming from. Closer up, I am able to make out what seems to be a glowing rock.

Mesmerized by this huge glowing rock, I stand and stare at it before suddenly finding myself reaching out to it. The second my hand touches the rock, the glow begins to intensify. The warmth is what surprises me first. I run my fingers over it's smooth surface, unable to bring myself to take my hand away, even as I feel it growing warmer.

The glowing heat that's growing stronger and hotter every second is starting to cause my heart rate to increase. My breathing is coming now in short spurts as my muscles contract. Although I realize I'm starting to go through a full-blown episode like I've done so many times before, I still can't bring myself to let go. The fire from deep within me begins to burn as I watch the glow coming from the rock slowly work its way through my hand then up my arm. This glowing light is actually going into my body. I slam my eyes shut as visions suddenly surge into my mind.

Large amber eyes, same hue as the glow, staring straight

at me. A man's face ... tears streaming down his cheeks. I blink and he's gone, replaced by a strikingly unfamiliar celestial horizon. Like nothing I've ever seen. I hear Sandy call to me and turn.

I'm back. Back in the cave. Whose thoughts were those? Not my own. But that was Sandy's voice I heard, I'm sure of it. Having gone through his change years ago, he was sent to protect me. To observe from afar until I needed him most, like all members of the Circle do for those with special abilities.

I think back on those blue-gray eyes, unwavering in his devotion to the people he cares about—to me. I wonder if I'll ever see him again. Did The Order, and their obsessive drive to control and protect the source, finally get to him?

I glance down and see that the amber glow has now spread over my entire body. My heart feels as though it's going to combust. I can hear its frantic beating, faster than would seem humanly possible. I'm panting, unable to catch my breath. The heat is becoming excruciating, but I still can't bring myself to let go of the rock. It sends forth a flash and visions flood my brain again.

I'm lying on my back as shimmering waves of fabric move all around me. Beautiful material of translucent amber. I reach out to touch the silky material but can't seem to grasp it. I stretch farther, my fingertips almost touching it. Almost ... I grab it. I'm standing now. Flowing fabric all around me, but in my hand is something that sends electricity coursing through my body. Its cool, hard metal feels familiar, intimate. I know this weapon even though I don't recognize it. He screams my name, startling me.

I'm back again. Back to the cave, the rock. Back to the burning I feel throughout my entire body. Still unable to will my hand away from this rock, I feel its connection to me.

Whatever is happening to me is inevitable.

I watch as the amber glow emanating from the rock begins to wane. As the light fades, my chest feels as though it's being scorched. The pain is overwhelming, and I find myself unable to control my screaming as my flesh burns. Through my anguish I watch as the glow from my chest grows brighter.

I'm blinded then by a flash of light as I'm thrown backward.

"Julian ... ugh, do you really have to stuff the whole sandwich in?"

He's grinning at me, mouth full, eyes twinkling mischievously. I can't help but laugh at the sight of him.

Turning to Aiden, I see he's laughing, too. Our eyes connect, and I feel instantly at peace.

"Why don't you guys come over this afternoon, you can help me figure out what to write my term paper on while you walk around my room and make fun of stuff?" I suggest, grinning at them.

Julian, laughing, says, "Jo, we can't. We're dead."

My eyes fly open. I'm in agony. My entire body feels as though I've been beaten. All I can do is lie here on the hard cave floor whimpering through the torment. The glow coming from my chest seems to be ebbing ever so slowly, but the dull burn continues.

I try to take a deep breath, but it hurts so much. Sobbing, I close my eyes and allow my mind to drift away, knowing that another type of torture will begin.

His kisses are soft and sweet, just what I need right now. He always knows exactly how to make all the pain go away, even if it is for just a little while. He stops and smiles down at me. Those beautiful brown eyes I live to see are looking back at me.

"I love you, Jo," he says earnestly. How long had I wished and dreamed he would say those words to me?

Sighing, I smile up at him before wrapping my arms around his neck. As I draw him to me for a tight hug, I whisper, "I love you, too, Mark."

He suddenly stiffens and pulls away. I open my eyes and see Sandy staring down at me.

I flinch and I take in my surroundings. I weakly try to lift my hand a little, but the pain causes me to drop it. I run my tongue over my dry lips, tasting something unfamiliar and sweet. My stomach roils in response. Turning over, I dry heave.

Finally, my body is able to relax and exhaustion takes over. Death, sleep, whatever it is takes over, and I welcome it.

It's so cold. A shiver runs through my body, and I stuff my hand in my pocket hoping to feel some amount of warmth. I feel it then, the picture. There's no need to take it out and look at it as its image is burned in my memory. Irina. I can see her face staring back at me. Her dark hair falling down around her shoulders in rich, silky waves. So much like Julian's, now that I think about it. The same deep-blue eyes and light skin. Why did I not notice the resemblance before? So alike, in more ways than I thought possible.

Awake, I lay on my stomach for a while trying to gather the courage to move toward the entrance of the cave. If I give in to this suffering, I have no doubt that this is where my life will conclude. Irina's face pops into my mind, and I feel my rage giving me the strength to move. To fight through the pain. To push my body and mind to the breaking point if necessary to get to her.

I crawl slowly on my belly, fingers digging into the floor of the cave to help move me along. With each agonizing inch, my body screams in protest. Light at the cave entrance keeps me moving. In just a few more feet, I'll be bathed in its complete embrace. Finally, I'm there, on the ground outside of the cave entrance basking in the sunlight.

Closing my eyes, I already feel stronger. I let my mind drift, all the while hoping that when I open my eyes again, my odds will have changed.

2

—

t's the rattle that wakes me. Even though I'm out of it, it
takes me only a second to recognize the thing that's lying
about three feet from my head, coiled and agitated. I study
the tan and brown patchwork and flat triangle-shaped head,
raised, seemingly ready to strike. While my mind processes
the fact that it's a rattlesnake, the first I've ever seen in real
life, I find myself easing away from it.

It strikes, fangs out, but I dodge the strike easily, then
grab it and fling it across the landscape. Shocked not only at
what I just did but at how I feel at this moment I look down
at myself incredulously.

I'm a mess—a disgusting, dirty, bloody mess. But I'm
not hurt.

I'm healed.

I run my tongue over my soft, moist lips still tinged with
that strange sweetness that made me so sick before. My stomach lurches. What was that?

Looking back at the cave, I see the charred bodies of two
of the guards lying by the entrance. I hear something, subtle
but definitely something. Senses heightened, I duck behind
the nearest tree. A breaking twig, a cracking branch, but
steadily, like a group is moving in unison.

All my instincts are screaming for me to flee, to take off
running and try to save myself, but I don't. I just push that
part of myself away, back to a place that has no use to me
anymore.

This is when I realize the magnitude of my change. I'm

stronger yes, but it's not the physical strength that I feel the most at this moment. My emotions seem dulled ... a change I welcome more than any other. After everything that I've gone through, all that I've lost, being able to feel in control of my actions, hell, even having a logical thought for once is such a relief.

I close my eyes and concentrate on the sounds coming closer. With my back to the cave, I hear them closing in. Stupid military tactics. Coming at me from all sides.

"Stay right where you are!" a man commands suddenly.

I'm frozen in place, eyes closed, listening as each one of them comes into the clearing. I can hear their movements as they quickly adjust their stances and guns. Funny, I wonder what they think as they stand there looking at the mess of a girl before them. How threatening could I possibly look?

"On the ground!" that same voice shouts.

I don't move, not even a flinch.

"I said, get the hell down on the ground!"

I can feel the darkness coming, the rage.

"I'm only going to tell you one more time!" he says and I hear his gun click.

My senses jolt and eyes fly open. He gasps as I stare right at him.

"What the hell?" he mutters under his breath, looking at me terrified.

There are seven men in all, three on either side of the one barking out orders. I can feel my fury building the longer I stand here looking at them, dressed in that all too familiar garb.

Suddenly, the man in charge motions to the three men to my left. Hesitantly, they come toward me, guns raised. Standing my ground, I just glare at them, waiting for their motivations to become lethal. I can see beads of sweat covering their faces as they nervously make their way closer to me.

When they get to within a few feet of me they stop, seemingly awaiting their next order.

There's a blur to my right, and then I feel something hard press against my temple.

"All right bitch, we're going to start doing things my way."

I don't even have to look to know exactly who it is that's towering over me with his gun pointed at my head ... Mitchell. The image of him shooting Maria point blank in the head flashes through my mind.

"You've been a real pain in my ass lately," he growls through clenched teeth. "If she so much as flinches, put a bullet in her!" he shouts to the other men as he lowers his gun and leans toward me.

I feel his hot breath against my ear as he whispers to me in a voice laden with disgust, "I saw what you did to that mama's boy. You try that shit with me, and I'll fill you with bullets."

He lingers by my head, slowly breathing in my scent. "I should kill you now. Hell, I'd love to ... but no, I'll wait. I'll let Irina run those tests and shit ... I mean, she's not the only one that wants to figure out what makes you tick."

My body stiffens at the mention of Irina and Mitchell pulls back. Raising my hand toward his chest, I feel it, the energy source, my weapon from within, shoot out as he's thrown back with such force he flies through the air. I take off as the bullets begin.

After a few minutes of running, I realize my surroundings have dramatically changed. I slow down and then stop altogether when I see where I am. Down the mountain and past the tree line. How could I have gone so far?

I don't seem any different. There's no glowing light, no weird racing heart rate ... nothing. I feel completely normal.

Like I did before all this crazy changing turned my world up-side down. For the first time in a while, I feel like my old self. But as I glance up at mountain range and take in the distance I've covered, I realize ... I'm not my old self. Not at all.

Relishing for a moment in the fact that Mitchell is gone, I think about what he said. I think about Julian, how be-trayed I felt. About the things he did, the people he killed just to have me for his own. I start to shake ever so slightly as I feel the rage begin to well up again. He deserved his fate—Mitchell, too.

I pull the picture out of my pocket and stare at it. There's only one other person that needs to be held accountable for their actions. As I gaze over her features, I wonder what she'll think when she discovers that I'm still free and that Mitchell is dead. I smile to myself as I realize how connected to her own survival she believes I really am. How it must just eat her up inside ... at least, I hope so.

I head toward the only place I know to be around here – the cemetery.

I could very easily pick up my pace and be there in minutes, but I'm reluctant. I hesitate, even as I feel the rain begin. Glancing up I see the sky's changing, pushing me on, telling me get on with it. I continue on until I finally see it up ahead, getting bigger in the distance.

Walking through the gates, my clothes cling to me as I slosh my way to the one grave I've visited before, Aiden's. My one true childhood friend. The sting of his death hurts less now; I feel so unfamiliar with that girl who was Aiden's friend. I'm only a fraction of that person now.

A few yards away I see two fresh grave sites and head over. I'm shocked when I see the headstones – my parents.' How long had I been up on that mountain ... in that cave? How long had it taken me to go through my change ... days, weeks?

The rain continues to come down. I see him then. Covered by a black poncho, hunched over, grabbing something off the ground. He's headed in the same direction I am.

"It's a shame about those two ... burning up in that house and all," he says.

I look over and meet the gaze of an old man. He looks away from me quizzically as I watch as raindrops pelt the poncho covering his thin, bent frame.

"Just had to come out here and collect these tools is all. Don't want 'em rusting up," he says then begins to walk away.

"Uh, sir. Were you here, I mean ... did you see their funeral?"

He turns around slowly while nodding. Avoiding eye contact altogether now, he says, "Their's was a fast one, too fast if you ask me. Barely cold, and they got them in the ground and buried."

The Order. Whatever it takes to cover their tracks.

"Funny too, cause done properly I reckon lots of folks would've come from all around to pay their respects ... him being a professor and all. Even so, there was still a few kids there. Kids about your age..."

Quickly glancing up and away, I can tell he's thinking back on the day as he looks around.

"They're still looking for the girl, though. From what I hear, someone done run off with her."

So I'm still being hunted. I'm sure he means the police are looking for me, but they're not the ones I'm worried about.

"You wanna come inside and get outta the rain a bit?"

Ignoring his question, I ask, "Any other recent burials?"

Rubbing his hand over his chin he says, "Well let me see, old Mr. Potter was buried last Tuesday."

"Any boys?" I ask almost too urgently.

He looks around like he's racking his brain to remember. "No, not that I can recall."

My pulse quickens at the news that Mark and Sandy might not be here.

"Just that girl, the blond one."

Could it be that they're all right? Sandy maybe, but Mark? I saw him stabbed with my own eyes.

Unless Ava sent him somewhere that could have—

My breath stops short at the image that pops in my mind.

Ava, young, sweet ... so much like a little sister to me. And different like me, except instead of being a total freak, she just has the added ability of transporting someone to another location by merely touching their chest.

Oh god ... Ava. The blond one... I can hear his words ringing in my head.

I remember what happened the last time I saw her. What I did.

Mark had been stabbed ... I couldn't control myself. I just couldn't. My whole world was falling apart, and I couldn't help it. I couldn't help but grab her along with everyone else in my psycho death grip.

"Yep, just the girl. She was laid to rest over there," he says pointing to an area fifty yards or so away.

"Thank you," I say my voice trembling.

He heads off, tools in hand, in the same direction he came from.

It only takes me a second to see the fresh grave. Running up to it, I stop short when I see her name.

Sahara Walker.

It's Sahara, not Ava.

Of course she's here. I killed her.

Something hard hits me across the head sending me

sprawling. Right before the blackness overtakes my senses, I see the old man standing far off to the side just staring. Just staring at something above me.

3

—

"TURN LEFT THERE," I HEAR A male voice say.
"All these damn dirt roads, how the hell do you keep 'em all straight?"

I feel the vehicle make a sharp turn and realize I must be in the back seat. Everything's dark. There's a bag over my head and my wrists are bound behind me with some sort of hard plastic.

I breathe slowly, trying to stay calm. How did I get here? I play back my memory from the cemetery. I vaguely remember seeing two guys a few yards away. Groundskeepers? Apparently not. Whoever they are, it doesn't matter. I got caught up in the moment and let my guard down.

"Slow down! Shit, where's that next turn? Yeah, there it is, turn left."

As the vehicle makes another hard turn, I slide down the seat, hitting my head against the door. Wherever it is they're taking me, they seem to be in a hurry to get there.

"What are we gonna do about that old man?"

"Who, Crowley? Everybody knows he's a senile old coot, always spouting off about one thing or another. Nobody'd believe anything he'd say."

"Yeah, well, good thing she showed up when she did, I was getting sick of waiting around that creepy place. Having to sit there all night in the friggin' dark."

"What we gonna do if she wakes up?"

"Relax, I tied her up good. Besides, that head guy ... the giant one, said her mojo don't work on us. I'm guessing that's why they hired us," he says and snorts.

"Yeah, but did you see the way those crazy SWAT guys looked when he mentioned her? No way some harmless little teenager could scare guys like that if she weren't some freak of nature or something."

"For god sakes, you idiot, shut up! Whatever she is, I don't give a shit. The way I see it, easy money. We hand her over, then get our loot and get the hell outta Dodge."

The giant head guy. They must be talking about Mitchell. I wonder what they'll do when they find out he isn't coming. My heart rate quickens at the thought. I begin to pull at my wrists but they sting in protest.

"There it is. Just pull around back."

I hear the loose gravel under the tires as the vehicle slowly makes its way around then come to a complete stop.

"What the...? I thought these people had money. This is a damn shack in the middle of nowhere."

"Yeah well, what ya expect, fucking wackos probably. Now shut up and help me get her in there!"

"Whatever man, but I don't like the looks of this. I feel like I'm stepping into some stupid slasher movie or something."

The door by my head opens, and I pretend I'm still unconscious. They drag me out and carry me just a few yards before I hear something start banging.

"Damn door! Here, take her while I open it."

One of them throws me over his shoulder while I hear the other beat at the clunky wooden-sounding door. It opens with a loud creak, and I'm carried inside. Even with a bag over my head, I can tell the air is musty in here.

"Where do I put her?"

"Just lay her on that table over there."

As he carries me over, the stinging in my wrists is becoming unbearable. I try to keep them locked together tightly so they don't keep rubbing against the plastic, but when he puts me on the table they catch on the edge. I wince ever so slightly, but just enough. Suddenly, the bag is yanked off of my head, and I blink as the world around me begins to come into focus.

"Well, hello little lady," a man with a whole row of brown teeth says to me, grinning.

"Get away from her! And why'd you take that bag off her head, she done seen you now, idiot."

"Just want'n to see the face that goes with that body," he says, eyeing me.

"Shut it, and get away from her. You know what he said."

"I know, I know. But I can still look, ain't no harm in that."

"Yeah, but look, don't touch, fool."

The one can't seem to take his eyes off me while the other just stands at a window pulling an old dusty checkered curtain to the side, looking out into the darkness. It's nighttime again. How long was I out?

"Damn girl, you are pretty! Look at her eyes. Ever seen eyes like that?"

"Would you shut up? Now get over here and keep watch. They should be here any minute."

After the man with the brown smile goes over to the window and peers out, the other quickly steals a glance my way before sitting down on the other side of the room. He seems almost frightened by me, and I wonder what he's thinking as he stares straight ahead at the door ignoring me.

I look around the room at what's left of a ramshackle old cabin. Surprisingly enough, there's electricity here and an old television in the corner. There's another room right off a makeshift kitchen that I suspect must be a bathroom or bedroom. Either way, it's sure not the Ritz.

"They're here!"

I look to the window and see the headlights. The man sitting down stands up abruptly, seemingly nervous all of a sudden.

"Yep, it's that black Hummer."

"Okay, okay! Now get the hell away from the window! We don't want 'em thinking we ain't professionals," he says anxiously.

The man walks away from the window and comes up next to me. Before the other guy can see what he's doing, he leans over me and smells my hair. I recoil from his stench.

"Get the hell away from her!"

Just then the door busts open and two guys come through. Same black military outfits I've grown accustomed to. That's when he enters, dominating the cabin the moment he comes through the doorway.

I just sit there, shocked. I killed him. Felt the stinging pressure erupt from my hand as I blasted energy into his chest. How can this be? Even if he is one of my kind, what I did to him still should have killed him. Right?

"We got her all tied up like you said. Shouldn't cause you any trouble. Now, if we can get what's owed to us, we'll be on our way."

Mitchell stares at me, searching. After a few seconds, he seems satisfied and looks toward his men.

"Give these men what we promised."

"Come with us," the first crony says and motions for the two men to follow him out.

Before leaving, the guy with the brown smile eyes me then says to his friend, "Man, I wish I could've gotten me get some of that."

Ignoring him, Mitchell glares at me.

"He's quite the charmer, eh?"

I just sit there wide-eyed.

I jolt when I hear gunshots ring out.

"Couldn't let a couple of human thugs go off to tell their friends, now could I?" Mitchell says. "I mean, we do have to preserve our kind, right?"

"What are you going to do with me?" I ask.

Anger flashes across his face.

He pulls a blade from a sheath on his pants. I recognize the odd-looking knife instantly.

He notices my recognition and smiles smugly. "You like this knife, huh?" he says running his fingers over it's blade. "Good eye ... this knife is special. It's made specifically to ... well, I guess you could say gut our kind."

Instinctively, I begin to tug on my restraints feeling them bite further into my wrists, causing me to wince.

"Thought you killed me, didn't you," he says eyes brimming with rage.

"Well, you didn't. What you did hurt like hell, though." He leans over and plunges his knife into my thigh.

I scream out as pain shoots through my entire leg.

"Just because I'm not going to kill you now doesn't mean I can't have a little fun," he whispers menacingly in my ear as he slowly pulls the knife back out.

Voice raspy with anger, he growls, "You think what that boyfriend of yours can do between those pretty legs is as good as it gets?"

I hold my breath, waiting. His massive frame towers over me.

"Not even close," he says lifting the knife now tinged with blood to my face.

Slowly, he begins to drag the knife down the side of my neck and onto my chest, leaving a deep scratch along the way. He hovers over me for a minute, blanketing me with his hot breath. I gasp when he leans over and begins to lick the edge of the scratch on my chest. Looking away from him, I'm repulsed as his tongue slowly follows the path back up to my neck.

Breathing heavily in my ear he growls, "Lets just say, there's much more to our abilities than what you've seen."

Reaching out he grabs my hair and pulls my head back. I don't make a sound, just stare up into his face, so wrought with rage. He glowers at me but pauses when our eyes connect. He quickly pushes my head away, and something in his look changes.

"You freak!" he says before turning his back on me and seemingly adjusting himself.

Relief floods me as I recognize the fact that his train of thought seems to have suddenly switched. The pain in my leg is starting to subside and I can only assume it's busy doing that speed-healing thing. Even so, whatever they have my wrists tied with continues to dig into me with even the slightest movement. I can feel the slippery wetness of my blood lubricating it.

When he turns back around he seems more in control but just as angry.

He begins to unbutton his shirt as I sit here, my mind filling with dread. He opens his shirt, revealing some sort of metal object covering his abdomen.

"Like my new armor? Yeah, had it made special. I've seen the aftermath of your handiwork."

"Where are you going to take me?" I ask, hoping to get him back to his original task.

"Ok, I'll bite," he says and smirks. "You see, the fact that you're now linked with that thing in the cave makes me ... uncomfortable. So I'll hand you over to the bitch, let her use her little geek squad to figure out what makes you tick, then when I find the answers I'm looking for ... I'll put you all down."

Standing up, he reaches for something behind him.

"If you so much as try any of your shit, I'll shove this into that pretty little chest of yours," he says showing me one of those Taser-type devices. A weapon The Order's scientists created just to kill our kind.

The door opens and one of his men walks in.

"Sir, the bodies and car have been disposed of."

Mitchell doesn't respond for a moment, just stands there looking at me ... contemplating. Then something changes in his expression and he starts walking toward the door where the other guy is just standing, waiting.

"Very good, now grab her and let's go," he orders and leaves.

Without looking at me directly, the man helps me down off the table. Surprisingly more gentle than I would have thought, he leads me out of the shack and up into the back seat of the waiting Hummer. Once I'm in, he walks around to the other side and gets in next to me. With the other crony driving, Mitchell climbs into the passenger seat and we're off, headed back down the dark dirt road.

Every bump we hit sends a jolt of pain into my wrists. I shift uncomfortably and the man next to me looks over. When our eyes meet, he quickly looks away, as if looking at me could cause death itself. That's when I figure it out. They're scared of me. That's why this guy doesn't want to be on my bad side. Mitchell's scared, too; it's just when he gets scared, he gets tyrannical.

The Hummer begins to shake, making a thumping noise.

"We have a blow out sir," the driver says as he tensely holds onto the steering wheel.

"Sure we do," Mitchell says sarcastically. "Pull her up

beside that cluster of trees straight ahead."

"Yes, sir," he says sounding somewhat questioning.

Looking back at the guy sitting next to me, Mitchell snaps, "She does anything other than sit there, you put a bullet in her head. We'll see how fast she heals from that."

The man nods, but I can tell by the nervous way he clears his throat he's hoping not to have to deal with me at all, much less shoot me.

When the Hummer stops, Mitchell cocks his gun then says to the driver, "Run out a hundred yards from the vehicle before sweeping back around. We want whoever this asshole is between us and this hummer. And remember, put 'em down first. If they're someone we want alive, they'll heal, and if we don't, then we'll zap 'em."

They both jump out and with surprising speed disappear into the darkness. The driver, having left his door slightly ajar, causes the inside light to stay on. The guy next to me curses under his breath at the fact that we are sitting here completely illuminated while it's completely dark around us. A moment goes by and nothing happens, no noise or movement of any kind. I just sit there looking out the window, knowing that the guy next to me is probably getting more trigger-happy by the second.

It starts out as a faint light off to my right, followed by a crack. The guy tenses, and when I look over at him he's staring past me in the direction of what has now become a firestorm of flashing lights. Sensing his anxiety increasing, I begin to turn slightly in my seat. If I can just get my legs around...

He notices and raises the gun, resting it on my temple. I freeze and close my eyes expecting at any moment to feel ... what? What does it feel like to get shot in the head? Healing or no, it's not something I'm wanting to experience.

Just then his door is yanked open, and I'm staring at the last face on earth I would have ever expected, but have wanted more than anything to see.

Mark.

He reaches for the man, but the guy's too fast and manages to whip his gun across Mark's face, sending him flying backward. Leaping out of the Hummer, the man lands on the ground right beside him. Raising his gun he's suddenly tripped up as Mark grabs his legs sending him face first onto the dirt road, the gun flying out of his hands. Mark scrambles up.

"Jo—"

Grabbed from behind, he's yanked back and thrown down to the ground. As my mind tries to wrap itself around what's happening, the man smashes his fist into Mark's face.

Although different from my usual emotional response, I feel myself react. The plastic binding that up to now has been nothing but a source of pain for me just melts away. Literally melts. A glob of gooey plastic falls to the seat as I jump out of the Hummer.

He's standing over Mark now, gun pointed at him, looking much more menacing than he ever did with me. Coward, I think as I reach out and grab him, swinging him around to face me.

It's my touch that does it. He starts to convulse as he stands there, wide eyed, spontaneously combusting as I watch, grasping him in an iron grip. It isn't until his clothing actually starts to burn that I let go. He crumbles to the ground, a mass of burning flesh.

I look over and see Mark watching me as he gets to his feet. It's the look in his eyes that sends relief coursing through me.

"Jo, are you all right?" he says as he comes toward me.

I quickly step away from him, afraid of what my touch may do, but I'm not fast enough ... he grabs me in a tight hug. I gasp before I realize all my expectations and fears are unwarranted. The only thing that passes between us is the realization that we're together again.

"Oh God, I was so afraid..." He pulls back and looks down at me. I can see the pain in his eyes, the fear of unspoken possibilities. As I gaze up at him, all my questions and uncertainties fade as I revel in the fact that he's alive. Alive and here now, with me.

"You can go ahead and get yourself right back in the Hummer, you little freak!" I hear Mitchell command.

I look over and see him with his gun aimed right at Mark. I start to move in front of Mark right as Mitchell shoots. The bullet grazes my side but finds its intended target. Mark grunts and doubles over.

"I'm only gonna tell you one more time to get in the vehicle, or the next bullet I put into your boyfriend will end him!"

I hear the bullet leave the chamber and move to put myself completely in front of Mark. My body tenses waiting for it to pierce my skin, but nothing happens. I look over and see Mitchell lying on the ground. That's when my eyes catch sight of him—Sandy, coming up fast.

He helps Mark to his feet then slings one of Mark's arms over his shoulder while I take the other one.

"We better get out of here. I'm not sure how fast he heals."

I realize he's talking about Mitchell and look over at his body still lying on the ground unmoving.

"They had one of those Taser things with them. Maybe you should—"

"Yeah, I have one, too, but it doesn't seem to be working.

With you around, I think..."

Mark grunts then as his arm slips off my shoulder and his body bends under his weight. Sandy manages to hold him upright until we get to his car. It's the same gray four-door silver Porsche I've come to associate him with. Running around to the other side I climb in the back seat as Sandy helps him get in. I scoot over as close to the window as I can so Mark has enough room. No matter how far I go, though, I don't think he'll ever be able to fit comfortably. His body just isn't made for sports cars. Even so, he crams in, and I cradle his head in my lap. Sandy jumps in the front and starts the engine. Our eyes catch in the rearview mirror for a moment before he looks away, peeling off down the dirt road.

I stroke Mark's head remembering the touch of his skin, the feel of his hair. So afraid I would never get to see him again; it's hard to believe I'm here now. He's here. We're both here—together.

Looking over at his shirt I see that it's stained with blood. I try to tear my eyes away but can't. I take a shallow breath as I think about what Mitchell said, that the next shot would end him. So that must mean this wound isn't fatal, that he's going to be all right.

"Hey you," Mark says surprising me.

I try to speak but nothing comes out. He's attempting to smile, to try to act like nothing's wrong so I won't worry. Even with a bullet in his side, he's trying to make me feel better, to take care of me.

Tears flow down my cheeks and fall onto his face. I reach down and brush them away. His look that assures me all my feelings for him are reciprocated.

The Porsche makes a sharp right and we're back on a main road. I can only assume we're headed to Sandy's cabin. I watch his face in the mirror, his perfect features so serious, focused. He stares straight ahead, seemingly lost in thought.

Having Mark here with me is more than I could have hoped for, but that Sandy is alive and well also—and that they are together—it's unconceivable to me.

I lean my head against the door. Although I'm tired, I'm afraid to shut my eyes, afraid of where my mind will go. I want to hold onto this reality as long as I can.

4

—

The engine cuts off and my eyes fly open. Right away, I recognize the cabin garage from when I was here before and notice the same black motorcycle sitting next to a small car that's covered and parked in the corner. I look down at Mark and he's smiling up at me. When our eyes meet, his expression changes slightly.

"Glad you got to rest a bit," he says.

Suddenly, I feel self-conscious. I've been through hell and back so I must look terrible. I shift uncomfortably in the seat, giving him a weak smile. Sandy opens the door and helps him out, while I try to get back some of the circulation in my legs.

Once inside, Sandy takes Mark into the kitchen. He clears off the table and has him lie back on it. He then lifts his shirt to take a look.

"You'll be fine, but I'm afraid I'm going to have to take the bullet out in here. It's the only room with adequate lighting."

"Yeah, ok. And man ... thanks," Mark says as he slowly sits up.

"Well, you might want to wait until I take it out to thank me," Sandy says and turns toward me.

He does a double take as if really seeing me for the first time, but quickly looks away.

"I have to get a few things from the other room. Try to get him to drink some water," he says and heads out of the room.

I head over to the refrigerator and open it and grab a bottle of water. I take the water over to Mark and realize he's watching me. He doesn't ask, even though I can see the questions in his eyes. He just takes the bottle and drinks.

His voice cracks as he says, "God Jo, you have no idea how worried I was. It killed me not to know where you were, if you were all right or..."

He lays back on the table then and closes his eyes but not before I glimpse a remnant of the pain he must have felt while we were apart. I know it all too well. The thought that he suffered in any way because of me is unbearable.

Sitting on the edge of the table, I take his hand and put it up to my face. It's so incredibly large, covering the entire side of my head easily. Closing my eyes I hold it there feeling his warmth. After a moment I gently brush my lips across his palm and feel him shudder. I open my eyes as his hand comes to life, pulling me toward him. He stops when our heads are only inches from each other. I stare down at the tear-streaked face of the one I love.

I'm the one that breaks the spell with a kiss that's anything but gentle. A kiss filled with my need to be with him. A kiss that escalates until I hear Sandy coming from the other room.

I jump up and away from the table just as Sandy comes into the kitchen. If he noticed anything, he doesn't let on. He just walks over to the counter and sets a tray down with a couple of sharp-looking instruments on it along with an array of liquids and rags.

Sandy eyes me and says, "Why don't you go ahead and wash up while we do this?"

"What ... no. You'll need my help."

"Listen Jo, I can do this, and to be honest there's no reason you have to be a part of..."

He looks at Mark then, and as if on cue Mark chimes in.

"Yeah Jo, I'll be fine. It's no big deal."

"No way, I'm not leaving you."

They seem to realize they had better change their tactics if they stand any chance of getting me to leave.

"Jo, really, I'll be fine. Besides, you really should go ahead and shower. I mean, you look like you've been hiking through the woods for days," he says shooting Sandy a grin.

Sandy laughs and says, "He's right, Jo. You are looking a little rough."

All I can do is stand there looking between the two of them as they smile at each other like they're part of some stupid fraternity prank. I glance down at myself, at the dirty pants and shirt. I reach up and feel my hair and pull out pieces of a crushed leaf. They're right, I must look like a backwoods crazy person.

"Yeah, I guess I could use a shower. But are you sure you can..." The thought of what Sandy is going to have to do to Mark makes me instantly queasy.

They exchange glances with each other.

"No, really Jo; I'll be fine. Besides, it'll be more sanitary if you aren't here," Mark says and winks.

I roll my eyes and head to the bathroom.

"You're always beautiful to me, though," I hear Mark yell out in a weak but humorous tone.

"Uh-huh," I yell back sarcastically as I start to climb the spiral staircase.

When I get to the top and walk into Sandy's bedroom, I think back to the last time I was up here. I blush as I remember him standing here nude, eyes wide with surprise. I quickly push the thoughts away as images of his masculine perfection resonate in my mind.

Walking into the bathroom I see my bag sitting on the

counter. The bag I packed when my worst fear was that I would hurt my parents by leaving to protect them. If only that was all that happened to them.

I turn the water on to let it warm up. I pull my clothes off as if they're burning my skin. It's strange how a second ago I didn't think too much of my discomfort, but now the dirt and grime on my skin and grunge in my hair is vexing me to no end. I jump in the shower and turn the water to the hottest setting I can stand. I grab the soap and scrub. Soon I'm covered in a thick musky lather. Sandy's soap. When I'm done in here, he and I will have more in common than just some DNA strands.

After I've washed my hair until it squeaks and when my body is bright pink from the rubbing, I determine I'm as clean as I have ever been and get out. Stepping out, I feel the cool tiles under my feet. I welcome the feeling as the entire room is filled with warm, moist condensation. Grabbing a towel off the rack I dry off and head to my bag, taking out a pair of jeans and a blue, tight-fitting tank top.

It's the underwear and bra that make me cringe. What exactly did I think I was going to be doing when I packed these things? I think back to when I bought them. It was after Mark invited me to prom. I went to one of those sexy lingerie places in town to pick something out to wear under my prom dress.

Cursing to myself, I slip the blue lacy duo on and look toward the mirror to see how ludicrous I look, but I can't see anything through the steam. Leaning in, I swipe the towel across the mirror and stare. It's mostly me, except for the fact that in my reflection the eyes are completely different. I stare, transfixed by their deep amber hue. They had begun changing a month or so ago, but now they're transformed.

I look . . . inhuman. I stare at them incredulously, unable

to wrap my head around what I'm seeing. I've lived my life blending, moving under the radar.

A mark on my chest catches my eye. Gasping, I recognize it immediately. It's one of the symbols I saw etched on the large metal circle hanging above the hearth in this cabin. I reach up and rub my fingers over the raised skin, like a brand. What does it mean? I step back and study it. About the size of my palm, it rests there like some arbitrary sign that I've been through hell and back. I throw my shirt on, covering it completely.

Now that's better.

I finish getting dressed and brush my hair, noticing how its long silky chestnut strands smell and look like mine again. My skin has the same flawless texture that all the others like myself seem to possess. One perk I guess of being a freak.

Everything seems quiet as I make my way back downstairs. I practically leap the rest of the way when I hear Mark grunt. I run to the kitchen to find Sandy helping him sit up. Hearing me come in, Mark looks up. "Wow, Jo ... you're beautiful."

I go over to him, feeling instantly anxious when I see all the blood.

"Mark, are you all right?" I hear myself ask, my voice trembling.

"Yeah, I'm fine. You missed all the fun. Doc here fixed me all up," he says, looking paler by the minute.

I shoot a panicked look at Sandy, and he comes over.

He helps Mark off the table. "We better get you to bed. You need your rest."

"I'll be fine," Mark says to Sandy once he's standing. Suddenly, his knees buckle underneath him and he starts to go down. Sandy grabs for him and his massive frame.

"I think I better help you, big guy."

He manages to help him up the stairs and into the bedroom with me following right behind. He sits him on the edge of the bed and then takes a step back. I immediately go to him and start taking his bloody shirt off. He falls back into the bed with a grunt. I move his legs around and take his shoes off. I start to take his pants off but realize he's already asleep, and without his help it's useless to try. Instead, I just plop down on the edge of the bed and look towards Sandy but he's already stepped out.

I sit and watch as Mark's chest rises and falls in a steady pattern. I feel like one of those new parents that hover over their newborn's crib checking, double-checking that their baby is breathing.

Taking his hand in mine, I kiss his palm again and hold it up to my face for a few moments, feeling his warmth and breathing in his scent. I sit like that for a while, savoring the time spent just watching him sleep. Pale and wounded, but alive.

Once I've convinced myself he's all right, I head to the stairs. I walk into the kitchen to find a sandwich Sandy has made me, which is sitting on the table with chips and a Coke. I smile to myself and wonder how he knew that was my favorite. I don't realize until I polish off everything in about a minute how truly hungry I was. Then it hits me how long it's been since I've eaten. Another consequence to my change?

I leave the kitchen feeling suddenly very sleepy. In the great room, I sink onto the buttery leather couch, studying the twelve symbols on the metal ring overhead. One of these symbols is the same as mine. But what does it mean?

I hear Sandy's voice coming from the next room, muffled.

"We incapacitated him, but he was there so I'd say it worked," I hear Sandy say.

I realize Sandy's on the phone. I zero in on the conversation, my hearing amplified.

"...was hit harder than I realized," the man says on the other end of the line.

"How many of us are left?" Sandy asks him.

"You don't want to know. Man, we're a damn skeleton crew."

There's silence for a moment before Sandy asks, "What about Gio?"

"Sorry, I just don't know anything yet."

Silence.

"Listen Sandy, I don't trust that asshole. You know he's the real threat now. I'd feel better if you brought her here sooner than later."

"I don't think that's a good idea. We'd be vulnerable there. Besides, we really don't know what information Mitchell has; we just know he wants Jo."

"Yeah, but that's why we need her here. She has insight into Mitchell and, hell Sandy, she's, well ... Jo. A changed Jo."

"Tom, we aren't having this discussion again. You know how I feel. I will not jeopardize her safety, not even for the cause."

"God damn it Sandy, she is the fucking cause!"

Sandy says nothing. Does he agree with this Tom? Am I the cause, whatever that really means?

After another moment of silence, I hear Tom sigh then say, "All right, all right ... it's a fucking lost cause with you. Who would have thought, you of all people." He snickers then. "Fine, just sit tight and I'll let you know when I hear something," he says then hangs up.

It hits me then who Tom is. I knew I recognized the voice. It's Tom Perlow, the football guy.

Mark and I met him briefly after discovering he has

abilities, too. He's north of thirty, but you'd never know by looking at him. Outdoorsy type with blond hair and the familiar flawless skin. He's very attractive, that is, until he opens his mouth. Then he's just another conspiracy weirdo.

"How's he doing?"

Startled, I look over and see Sandy eying me, searching for answers that have nothing to do with Mark.

"He's resting," I say sounding depleted.

"Don't worry Jo, he's strong. It's just, losing more blood after what Julian..."

I stiffen at the mention of his name and stand motionless as the memories begin to creep in.

"Ava! Where—what happened?"

"She's fine. She's with Tom, safe."

"Tom? The same Tom that was on the phone just now?" I say, hearing the rising panic in my voice. "The one you said was somewhere unsafe?"

Ava's not my actual sister, but it doesn't mean I don't feel responsible for her. She looked up to Sandy and I as if we were her family, caring for her, protecting her. How could I not feel the weight of that responsibility now?

"I know what you heard," he says oddly not surprised that I was able to hear the conversation. "She's safe with him, but Jo, you have to understand it's very different for you. Mitchell is after you and until we can figure out what's going on with him—and with you, too—it's just better for us to stay here."

"But if anything happens to her–"

"Jo, don't worry, she's going to be fine. Tom will take good care of her. Plus, you should probably think about staying put so Mark can heal," he says as his eyes avert my gaze.

He's right, Mark isn't like us. He'll need time.

Sandy must know that mentioning him sealed the deal

for me. I'd never consider putting Mark in harm's way. It's the same way Sandy thinks about me.

"Why is this old football guy Tom involved anyway?" I ask.

"Tom knows just about everything there is to know about our kind. Within the Circle, I guess you would consider him our leader. Most people thought Adrian, the one calling all the shots at the mission, was actually running things, and that's the way Tom liked it. He's smart and he knows things ... I don't always know how, but he does. He's the one that told me not only to trust Mark but to help him. Of course, that was after he helped us to get out of that hospital, then find you."

"Tom? Really? He seemed so ... odd," I say, picking the nicest of all the words that jump in my head.

"Yeah, I guess he is," he says and smiles. "He can be a bit rough around the edges. But the way he can read people, know what they're going to do, it's amazing. I've never seen anything like it. Of course, that was only until he met you."

"Me?"

"It's different with you. He hasn't been able to ... know your intentions as well as well as he can with others."

"But you know my intentions," I ask feeling instantly insecure.

He steps toward me and the urgency of his voice surprises me. "Jo, what happened to you when you left? Where did you go? I was going crazy trying to figure out—"

"Sandy, I'm fine," is all I can mutter as my heart is slammed with an overwhelming urge to throw my arms around him and hold on for dear life.

"You seem different, I mean you look ... different," he says looking at my eyes.

I want to tell him. I need to, but I can't bring myself to

go there right now. I absentmindedly rub my hand over my freshly branded skin.

"Oh my god, Jo! What is that?" He reaches for my shirt to get a better look, but instinctively, my arm shoots out.

My eyes slam shut as electricity fires through my body. I feel the heat but am unable to control myself.

Suddenly, there's a flash and then darkness.

I open my eyes to find myself standing on a massive stone ledge. The entire thing is made of a strange metamorphic rock with mirror-like fragments throughout. Instinctively, I take a few steps back away from the edge, but then stop as a strange sensation begins to flow through me. I want to stay here, to feel this way forever, but it's the light, the sparkling light I catch sight of off to my right that draws me away. I walk towards it.

Then he's there, right before me ... perfection in every sense of the word. My eyes roam slowly over the flawless bronzed skin of his bare stomach and chest. He takes a step toward me and I can sense all of him now, every flex of a muscle, every slight movement. I can hear his heart rate increasing to match my own. I can feel him breathing, reacting in the same way I am.

Every instinct is telling me to reach out to touch him, kiss him ... consume him. Every fiber in my being is screaming for me to.

"Sandy...," I hear myself say in a husky voice that sounds nothing like my own.

It's his screaming that jolts my senses. I find myself back in the cabin still grabbing his arm, but with my other hand now pressed hard against his chest.

I instantly break the connection, and he's violently thrown back away from me. Shocked and panting, I stand there watching him lying on the floor gasping for air, his chest emitting an all too familiar glow.

What have I done?

He looks up at me and my own shock is mirrored in his expression.

Gasping, he croaks, "Your eyes!"

The look on his face is alarming. I run to a mirror. What I see reflected back at me is unbelievable. My eyes have now morphed into something that could not possibly be from this world.

My eyes are ruddy amber with some sort of black pattern in the center. Even so, it's not how they look that freaks me out the most, it's the fact that they ... move. It's as if they have a life of their own.

I turn around to find Sandy catching his breath. He's sitting up seemingly lost in thought as he stares straight ahead. I hurry to him, kneeling beside him.

I can't even say the words. I feel so horrible about what I did to him that I just bury my face in my hands and start weeping. How could I hurt him when all he's ever done is help me?

"Jo," he says pulling my hands away from my face. As I stare into those blue-gray eyes so full of concern, I know he's done much more for me than help me. He's loved me.

"Jo, are you all right?"

How can he ask me that, I mean come on...

"Me? I'm the one that hurt you, dummy," I manage to stammer out.

He laughs. "Yeah, well, I think I'll live."

"I'm so sorry," I say and throw my arms around his neck for a tight hug. As I brush against his chest, he flinches. He pulls up his shirt. There above his heart, in precisely the same place as my own, is a freshly branded symbol.

"What the hell..."

It's not the same symbol as mine, but it's one of the twelve. I did this. I branded him. Why? What does it mean … a connection, like I felt with the meteorite? How am I connected to Sandy?

"Jo, how did you…"

"I didn't. I mean, I didn't mean to. I have no idea why … or how…"

I can feel the tears coming again but I push them away.

"Listen, I'm all right."

"Sandy, I didn't mean to—"

He hugs me. "Jo, don't worry about it, I know you'd never hurt me. I just wonder what it means?"

I glance at his brand and cringe. The skin, raised and red, is already looking less horribly painful than it did even a minute ago.

"Does it hurt?" I ask, already knowing the answer but needing to make sure.

"No, I guess it's already healing."

With his usual way of trying to ease my concerns he says, "I kind of like it."

I just look at him like he's full of it.

"No, really," he says laughing. "I can't say I've ever had a girl give me a gift quite like this before."

I tell him all about my change, leaving out anything pertaining to the visions. I figure it's probably better to keep those to myself for now.

I tell him about the differences I feel within myself now. How my mind seems sharper, clearer. How my emotions seem more in check.

I don't tell him how truly different I do feel. That deep down I know I'm not completely human anymore. I know it. I've changed into something very different. I think about my last vision then and, blushing, look away when our eyes meet.

"I better go check on Mark," I say suddenly and jump up, leaving Sandy staring after me as I make an awkward escape.

5

—

"I REALLY DO THINK MY FAVORITE THING to do is watch you sleep," Mark says and kisses me tenderly. His lips, warm and soft, instantly awaken more than my consciousness. Wrapping my arms around his neck, I pull him down.

"Whoa ... whoa, uh ... I'm afraid my side's still a little ... sore," he says laughing. "I do enjoy your enthusiasm, though."

"Sorry, guess I'm just trying to make up for lost time," I say grinning.

"Oh, we'll make up for lost time, all right. I just want to be functioning at a hundred percent when we do."

"Well, I'll take you any way I can get you," I say pulling him down for a much gentler kiss.

For the next few minutes, we just lay there, in each other's arms, relishing in the fact that we're together again. I wonder then how long it's going to take me to shake this feeling of uncertainty about our future together. I'm so afraid I'll lose him. That I'll wake up and it's all just part of a crazy vision. A figment of my subconscious ... the part that harbors all my hopes and dreams.

"You all right? You seem ... somewhere else," he asks looking concerned.

"I guess I'm just having a hard time wrapping my head around all this," I say.

He suddenly sits up and in a serious tone says, "Jo, I'm not going anywhere. You don't have to worry about that. I won't lose you again."

I believe him. I don't doubt a word he says or at least the fact that he means it. It's everything else that feeds my uncertainty. Those things I just can't seem to control.

"But what if I'm not the same person I was ... before."

"You've changed, I know, I see it. I mean, I see the physical changes sure, but you're still the same Josephine I fell in love with. The same person who took my breath away every time I saw you at your locker. That would get my heart racing with just a ... well, pretty much anything you do gets my heart racing," he says and laughs.

Tears sting my eyes and his tone changes.

"Jo, all I'm saying is you're still the person I love more than anything in the world, and no matter what happens that will never change," he says then kisses me. Smiling mischievously then he adds, "By the way, I think your new eyes are cool."

Shocked, I pull back. "So you have noticed!"

"They're a little hard not to notice. I mean, I've never seen anything like it before. Like you, beautiful and unique ... perfect."

All I can do is stare at him in disbelief. He's so casual, so calm about it. How can he be? I mean, I saw how he reacted when I killed Sahara.

"But, when I ... when Sahara died, you could barely look at me, and now you think it's all ... ok?"

Pain crosses his face. "Jo, I'm so sorry ... I don't know how I'll ever make it up to you. I never should have reacted that way ... ever."

"I think your reaction was pretty appropriate actually. It's the reaction I'm getting from you now that's making me uncomfortable."

He smiles slightly before saying, "Yeah, I guess I had to play catch up pretty fast. Once I got a glimpse of my life without you, though, everything changed. At that point I didn't care about all the other stuff, I just knew I wanted you. After that, it was easy."

"So Sandy told you everything?"

"Yep. He's a good guy. He seems to really care about his ... causes."

I wonder then how much he knows about Sandy's true feelings. Regardless, he knows I love him, and that's all that matters, right? A pang of guilt hits me then as I think about all that Sandy has done for me ... for us.

As images of what happened last night creep into my mind I quickly change my thoughts, blurting out the first thing that comes to mind. "How did you know where to find me?"

"What?" he asks looking at me quizzically.

"On the dirt road, when those men had me?"

"Oh, right. Sandy got a call, some old guy at the cemetery said you were there. By the time we got there, you were gone. How he knew where to go after that, I really don't know. He talked to someone on phone. Sandy can be as mysterious as he wants, just so long as we got you back safe."

"That you did," I say smiling as I push him down on the bed. He grunts then and I quickly sit up alarmed.

"What is it?"

"It's nothing, just still a little sore," he says and tries to give me his most convincing smile. It doesn't work.

"Let me see your side," I say a little more authoritatively than I would want to, but feeling slightly shaky.

He lifts his shirt and I see that the bandage is soaked with blood.

"I'm going to get Sandy," I say abruptly, then jump up and head downstairs to the kitchen. Sandy's voice comes from behind me.

"Jo, what's wrong?"

"It's Mark. He's still bleeding," I say hearing the alarm in my voice.

He nods and we're upstairs in an instant. Mark's standing by the bed and seems a little embarrassed when he sees Sandy.

"Really, I'm all right. Just need to throw on another bandage," he says nonchalantly, purposefully not looking my way.

Stepping toward him I say, "Mark, you're still bleeding. Just let Sandy take a look, please."

He succumbs and lifts his shirt showing us that he's already pulled the bandage back himself to take a look.

Sighing he looks at me sweetly. "See Jo, I'm fine. The stitches are still intact. I just need another bandage."

Sandy turns to me and in a calm manner says, "It's okay, Jo, he's right. He's not going to heal the way we would."

Sandy, thinking I'm reassured says, "I'll go get a new bandage," then heads out the door.

I smile sweetly at Mark but know it's more than our differences in healing that has me worried, much more.

Pushing the food around on the plate, I try to calm my stomach. Another sandwich, another success making my favorite. This time though, any hunger I feel is taking a back seat to the crazy thoughts that have been running through my head all day.

Why did I brand Sandy, and why the vision? Why that vision? If things weren't complicated enough.

Mark's been resting off and on while Sandy seems to be going out of his way to put some distance between he and I.

He's probably wondering what I really did to him. Keeping a distance in case I suddenly get another urge to do something else.

Sandy's phone suddenly comes to life, breaking the funk in the room. Looking at the screen, he glances at me then quickly jumps up.

Mark walks in just as I push away from the table and my plate of uneaten food. Sandy's normally calm demeanor is replaced by a sudden sense of urgency. He quickly heads to the other room as I follow right behind, bombarding him with questions.

"What's going on? Who was that?"

Sandy seems almost perplexed as he ignores me and takes a black duffle bag out of a closet and starts looking through it.

"Where are you going ... Sandy!"

Looking up at me he seems to gather his wits and says hurriedly, "Sorry Jo, it was just a text from Gio."

"A text? Sandy, where are you going?"

"Jo, I'm sure it's nothing, but she left me a code. A code to meet at my place in the city."

"Your place in the city?"

"Yeah, I own a place in the Braddock Building. The text was a code we set up in case anything like this ever happened. A way to get a message to the other to meet there."

"Sandy, you can't just go. I mean, what if it's a trap or she's tricking you or something?"

"Listen Jo, I've known Gio for a long time. She wouldn't betray me. If she left the code, it means it's urgent," he says and zips the bag up and grabs another small one out of the closet and heads to the door.

How can he have such blind faith in that girl? Grabbing his arm, I find myself almost pleading, "Sandy, please. At least let me come with you."

Mark steps forward suddenly, "Jo, I don't think that's a good idea."

"He's right, you can't come. We need to keep you out of harm's way until we know exactly what's going on," Sandy says trying to sound reasonable.

"But you can't go alone," I say.

"I'll go with him," Mark says all of a sudden.

"No!" Sandy and I say in unison.

Sandy looks at Mark, who's scowling now. "Look, you really shouldn't be up and around too much." Then turning toward me he sighs, "Besides, this isn't my first walk in the park. Trust me Jo, I know what I'm doing."

Then before I have time to answer, he's past me and out the door in an instant. Damn that quick speed thing. I start to go after him, but Mark grabs my arm as I hear the Porsche start up with its usual purr.

"Mark, we can't let him go alone!"

"Jo, we don't really have a choice."

I think then about the Braddock Building. It's one of the most luxurious buildings in our city. A loft or condo in there would cost you an obscene amount of money. I'm reminded of Sandy and his seemingly unlimited funds.

"We have to do something. We can't just let him go alone, no matter what he says," I say pleadingly. Maybe a little too pleadingly by the look on Mark's face.

"I'm sure he'll be fine. He's as capable a guy as I've seen."

"You're right," I say changing my expression suddenly. "I'm sure he'll be fine. Come on, let's get you back to bed," I say smiling and then head upstairs. He eyes me suspiciously but follows.

After I get him somewhat settled, I run back down to get him some water, knowing the entire time my intentions are anything but sincere. I head to the garage where Sandy's motorcycle and covered car are parked.

Grabbing the keys off the hook, I realize they're only for the black motorcycle in the corner. No way.

I head over to the car and rip the cover off. It has to be one of the coolest little cars I've ever seen. An Alfa Romeo Spider in bright yellow. The kind of car the boys in school would get excited just thinking about. Where did Sandy get all his money?

I flip the visor down but no key. I glance around the seats and in the glove box, but no luck. Where could he have put it?

I don't have time to find it, so I gather my courage and head toward the motorcycle.

"Do you have any idea how to drive that?" I hear Mark say from behind me.

Startled, I swing around and see him standing there eyeing me.

"Jo, come on. You really think I'm that big of an idiot. Going to get me a glass of water," he says and laughs.

"Mark, I just can't..."

"I know Jo," he says then eyes the yellow car. "I say we take that."

"I could only find these," I say holding up a set of keys with the same logo as the motorcycle.

He smiles mischievously as he walks by me, taking the keys and hopping on. "I'd rather take this anyway."

I open the garage as he starts it up. The sight of him sitting there, his huge frame a commanding presence on top of the motorcycle, sends a quiver through me.

"What about your side?" I ask loudly, suddenly worried again.

"Don't sweat it. Now put that helmet on and let's go."

"There's only one. What about you?"

"Jo, I'm not going to argue with you," he says giving me a look that my concern for him is getting tiresome. I strap on the helmet and get on behind him.

"Now hold on!" he shouts over the roar of the engine as he revs it and takes off.

As we speed along, I can tell he's done this before. The ease with which he shifts the gears, leans into the turns. With my arms wrapped around him in a vise grip, I would normally feel exhilarated, but I can't stop worrying. Worrying about him and the fact that he shouldn't be on the motorcycle to begin with, especially without a helmet. Also worrying about Sandy and all the trouble he could be getting himself into.

As if reading my thoughts, Mark shifts the gear suddenly, kicking up the speed.

Against a shadowy mountainous backdrop, the city suddenly rises up out of the desert as the setting sun silhouettes its skyline. Slowly twilight shifts into night as we move closer to the city limits. Coming up on the city itself, my eyes are drawn to the marvel that is the Pym Tower. Right next to the Braddock Building, it's impressive.

The road suddenly widens as the lanes multiply around us. The city's known for its broad streets lined with palms transplanted from a faraway land. I glance up at the stories of dark tinted windows looming over us. Just ahead to the left is the entrance to the underground parking garage for the Braddock Building. Although there's topnotch valet parking on the ground level, the parking garage is the best way to get into the building unnoticed.

Mark suddenly slams on the brakes just as Sandy's silver Porsche blasts out of the entrance and abruptly turns heading away from us. Before my mind's able to grasp what I've just seen, a black car emerges right behind him with the same gusto. But it's when this car suddenly stops short and I'm able to really get a good look that I realize where I've seen it before. A sleek muscle car, ominous with its black tinted windows and exterior. It's the same black car from my accident, the one that seemed out to get me the night I took a drive along the mountain road.

Now it's headed in our direction weaving through the oncoming traffic.

"Mark! That's the car from—"

Mark takes off down a side street. Tires squealing, I look back just in time to see the car fly in reverse and maneuver itself after us. The person driving definitely knows what they're doing.

Mark glances back and twists the hand grip. The motorcycle revs in response then lurches forward as he shifts gears. As we speed down the darkened side street, I can see the main road coming up fast. A cluster of cars whiz by, all traveling in the opposite direction of the road we were last on.

Mark slows to make the sharp turn left, and as he does the black car comes racing up behind, quickly closing the gap between us. Just as the car is about to slam into the back of the motorcycle, Mark downshifts and puts his left leg on the ground as a balance, tires smoking. He somehow manages the drastically sharp turn, putting us on the main drag. The car, unable to make the turn completely, shoots out of the side street, glancing an oncoming pickup truck. The car, barely inhibited by the crash, promptly gains speed again as the truck veers to the side, a crumpled mess. I realize immediately we aren't dealing with an ordinary car.

Having gained a little ground, we speedily weave through the traffic. A horn honks as we pass within a foot of a white work truck. I'm amazed at the ease with which Mark is able to maneuver the bike, but even so, the black car is catching up.

"Hold on," Mark yells suddenly.

Before I'm barely able to respond, he turns the bike slightly to the left, slams on the brakes, and makes a sharp left turn down another side street. The car goes speeding by.

Mark accelerates, knowing this is probably the best chance we're going to have to get away. Looking back, that's when I see it. Sandy's silver Porsche.

"It's Sandy," I yell to him over the whirring sound of the motorcycle. He glances back and then slows up. Sandy drives up beside us as Gio, sitting in the passenger's seat with the window down, motions for us to stop beside them.

Not surprisingly, Gio's as gorgeous as ever. Long thick hair as dark as night, with eyes to match.

We're on a narrow poorly lit side street that runs between the two main streets.

"Get back to the Braddock Building and meet us in Sandy's loft. Number 3210, door code 1200," Gio hastily says, then seems to take a double take as she sees my eyes.

Looking past her, I say to Sandy, "It's that same car from the mountainside, the one that—"

"Yeah, we know. Must be The Order. They probably followed me when..." then he glances over at Gio.

"It's back," Mark yells then and I turn to look. Sitting motionless on the edge of a side alley, the car seems as though it's waiting. But waiting for what?

My senses catch it before my thoughts do. I instinctively draw my head back just as two metal discs fly by, missing me by an inch but instead lodging themselves in Gio's head. I stare in horror as she yells out just as I hear Sandy shout for Mark to go.

We take off again. Mark takes a sharp turn getting us back on the main road and we head back toward the Braddock Building. Racing along, there's less traffic on this street so he's able to kick it in to high gear.

As we speed along, I close my eyes, concentrating on the discs that had most likely missed their intended mark. Pewter-colored metal, lined with oddly serrated, lethal-looking edges. I even caught a glimpse of a strange symbol, like something from the Far East.

We're coming up on the parking garage, and I still don't see the black car. I think about Sandy, who we left behind with a wounded Gio. I hope he didn't do anything I'm going to regret.

Mark quickly turns the bike onto the steep down ramp leading into the immense underground parking area of this huge downtown residential skyscraper. He drives right up to the glass doors of the entrance into the building. Although the parking garage is nothing special, the area surrounding the entrance oozes luxury. I get the impression that once we enter those doors, our environment is going to drastically change.

Mark parks the motorcycle and I hop off. Sandy flashes in my mind as he's getting off the bike.

"I think we should go back—"

I hear it then, the all too familiar acceleration of a certain engine, an engine that belongs to a car that will no doubt become a major player in my nightmares.

I shoot a look at Mark and we take off running for the doors. I pull the handles—the doors are locked.

What the hell do we do now? I stand there running through various options for smashing the glass. Mark, using his brain and the keypad situated on the side of the door, punches in the code Gio gave us and we're through, just as the black car explodes into the garage.

As we run around the corner and down a short hallway headed for the elevators, I catch sight of dimly lit sconces, casting a muted light that reflects off the perfectly polished marble floors. I glance up at a sign directing us to the elevators and spa.

The spa. Ha. Maybe in another life.

Making our way to the elevators, we have to run around a tremendous flower display on top of a rather ornate-looking table. Getting to the doors, I immediately push the Up button, all the while listening for any indication that someone could be approaching.

Ding ... the doors open without delay. In the doorway eyeing us curiously is an elevator attendant.

"What floor please?" he asks as we step in.

You've got to be kidding me. I've just been in a race for my life, but I can't push a button to operate an elevator? I'm instantly irritated.

"Thirty-two" I say unenthusiastically.

"Floor thirty-two, my pleasure," he says staring straight ahead at the numbers and thankfully ignoring us.

That's when I look over at Mark to roll my eyes, but notice instead how pallid he is. I gasp, causing the elevator guy to briefly look my way. He gives me an odd look, but I don't care. All I care about at that moment is the fact that all down the side of Mark's shirt is blood. Now getting to Sandy's loft has become even more urgent for me.

Mark, knowing my thoughts, gives me a weak smile just as the elevator dings again and the doors open. He steps out and as I follow, the elevator attendant, in the most surprisingly slick manner, places something in my hand as he says, "You have a good night, Jo."

What the...

The doors close with that same telltale ding. Then he's gone and I'm left with an all too familiar feeling of being a pawn in a game where I don't know the rules.

Clutching the key he just gave me, I start looking for loft number 3210.

6

——

The key works perfectly. With Mark looking paler by the second, whatever this stupid game is, I decide, I'll play it.

Agitated but mostly worried for Mark, I go through the door first, not knowing what or who we might find. On edge, senses heightened, I flip a wall switch just inside the door and stand, taken aback by what I see.

The place is right out of the 1960s. Modern and geometrical, with a retro feel. Resting on the shiny onyx-like floor in the center of the room is a funky glass coffee table in front of two white leather couches. Couches that look like the last thing I'd actually want to sit on. Dispersed throughout the large room are sculptures, each piece placed high up on freestanding pedestals.

"Oh...k," Mark says looking around with my same expression of disbelief. "Sandy owns this?"

I shrug.

Over to the side tucked away in a cove, seemingly all to itself, is a black grand piano resting on top of an extravagant shaggy white rug. Pure opulence.

Toward the back of the room are three steps leading to a rather large tinted window. In front of the window is by far the strangest thing I've seen yet. A telescope. On the side of the scope is a cabinet. Not the chic-looking one that you would expect given the motif of the apartment, but a strictly utilitarian one. The military-grade cabinet and scope just add to the oddness of this place.

Feeling as though I just stepped into a bad 007 meets Elvis movie, I'm beginning to wonder if I know Sandy at all. The cabin decor matches his personality perfectly, but this...

I head for the bathroom medicine cabinet looking for anything that can help Mark. I smile then when I open the lower cabinets to find a whole slew of medical supplies. I may be questioning Sandy's sense of taste but not his preparedness.

Grabbing just about anything and everything, I call out to Mark as I walk back into the bedroom. He's already there, leaning forward as he sits on the edge of the mattress.

"Are you okay?" I say searching his face as I kneel down in front of him. Noticing my concern, he immediately perks up.

"I'm fine, really. Just got a little winded, that's all," he says, clearly lying for my benefit.

Grabbing a box of bandages, I fumble around with it trying to get it open as my hands tremble. I saw all the blood on his shirt in the elevator, so I know his winded excuse is crap.

"Jo," he says eyeing me strangely.

I avert his gaze as I start to feel the inner sting of an impending emotional breakdown. That weirdo with the discs, the whole motorcycle chase ... our life together just can't seem to not have a level of danger involved. For me, it's one thing, but for Mark it's another altogether.

"Jo, really ... I'm fine," he says more seriously this time searching my face as if trying to read my thoughts.

We stay like this for a moment, savoring our connection, our love for each other. Suddenly his look changes, sending a jolt of electricity through my body. Bending down his lips touch mine, soft at first but quickly changing in intensity. Pulling me toward him, he slowly falls back on the bed until I find myself lying on top of him, his kiss unexpectedly increasing in urgency.

Any thoughts I had just a moment ago about him being hurt or getting hurt quickly dissipate as I feel his large muscled frame pull me tighter to him. Even injured, bleeding, he's only human.

My thoughts are fleeting as the need I feel for him takes over completely. In all the times I've imagined us being together finally, I never pictured it being so on a whim, so spur of the moment.

Reaching down I grab at his shirt. As soon as my hand touches the slick wetness of his blood, I push away from him and gasp. Blood has completely soaked through the bandage and is all down his side.

"We shouldn't have ... your injury..." I say shakily and start bungling around again with the boxes of bandages.

I tear open one of the packages. All the sanitized bandages spill out onto the bed. "Damn."

"Oh hell, it's not that much blood. I'm a big guy, so I gotta lot to spare," he says suddenly looking concerned about me.

Mark grabs his shirt and pulls it off. "Hey, do you think you could grab me some water?"

"Oh my gosh, of course," I say and bolt out of the room.

Getting to the kitchen I hurry to the refrigerator hoping to find a bottle of water. It's not just one that I find, but two shelves full. Other than the water the entire refrigerator is empty. Obviously Sandy hasn't cooked anything here in a while.

Grabbing a bottle, I take it back to the room and find Mark is gone. He's in the bathroom with the water running. I knock on the door.

It opens and he's standing there smiling with a new bandage pressed to his side. "See, good as new."

"Why does it keep bleeding like that if it's all stitched up?"

"I guess I'm supposed to take it a little easier than I am."

"Then that's exactly what you're going to do! You're going to stay here–"

"Hey ... hey," he says trying to calm me as he steps closer. "I'll lose every bit of blood I have before I take my eyes off of you again."

"That's ridiculous."

"No, it's fact. You're not going to run off leaving me wondering where you are, if you're all right. No, not again," he says with an edge to his voice.

He's upset, maybe blames himself for what happened before. I don't know, but whatever he thinks he seems determined, so I quickly change the subject.

"Does your mom know where you are?" I ask when her face, so much like Mark's, is the first thing to pop in my head. The talk of the town, first when her husband all of a sudden left without a word, but lately because of her way of coping it ... the occasional benders. Regardless, she's always seemed a sweet, warm person to me. At least someone that loves her sons, that I know.

He smiles knowing exactly what I'm trying to do. "She knows I'm safe. Sandy and I decided it was best for her and Harrison if I stuck with him. But until we found you, he would've had a hard time getting rid of me anyway."

I think of his younger brother, Harrison. Fifteen years old and not only has his father left, now the older brother he's always thought the world of has, too.

Just then I hear the front door open. It's Sandy and Gio, and by the looks of it, her head wounds are already healing. She's holding one of the metal discs in her hand, manipulating it so that the serrated blades pop in and out by just a push of a button. Making the disc small and smooth edged one minute and much more lethal another. Seeing how sharp

68

the edge is up close sends chills through me when I think of it piercing the poor girl's skin.

My feeling of genuine concern for her is immediately squashed though when I see her eyeing a bare chested Mark. Why does she constantly lust after him, even in front of me?

"She insisted on following you," I hear Mark say to Sandy as they stand glaring at each other.

Sandy snaps back. "To put her in danger—"

"Whoa! You just took off knowing she'd never let it rest, she'd want to come after you! What was I supposed to do?"

"Stop her!"

"Oh really..." Mark scoffs. Sandy, I'd like you to meet Jo..."

"Guys, stop! I know you're both trying to look out for me, but I'm not going to just stay put. Just stand back while everyone I care about gets hurt. Sandy, you were right to help Gio. It's who you are and I wouldn't expect you not too, but like Mark said, there's no way I'd let you go without help. Think what you want about me, both of you ... but I'm different now. I can do things, probably more things than I realize, so why don't we spend less time protecting me and more time trying to figure out my abilities. Hell, I may be some alien superhuman weapon," I say throwing my hands up in exasperation. "I mean, don't you two ever watch TV?"

Mark smiles and Sandy sighs, seemingly less convinced.

Turning his attention to Sandy now, Mark says sarcastically, "By the way, cool digs."

With a hint of humor, Sandy looks around. "Yeah, I bought this place as is. I never come here, but Tom does. He uses it for surveillance," he says and motions to the telescope.

"Who is he watching from here?" I ask.

"The Order. They rent offices in the top three floors of the tower, under the name of a bogus research and development company."

"So that's where the people that want to get their hands on Jo are? The next building over?" Mark asks incredulously.

"Yeah, well it's also Tom's HQ."

I'm flabbergasted. "In the same building?"

"Yeah, I know. Welcome to Tom's quirky sense of humor. I thought it was crazy, too, at first, but honestly when you think about it, it's genius. I mean I have to say, it's helped a lot with gathering intel."

Mark chimes in, "So what kind of equipment do you have here?"

Sandy walks over to the cabinet and punches in some code before the door makes a loud click. He swings the doors open, revealing a large assortment of complicated-looking gadgets and gizmos. Things you would expect a secret agent to have concealed in some special hidden room down in his so-called wine cellar.

I shake my head, taking a mental note that I need to stop watching spy shows.

"Oh, man ... look at this stuff," Mark says headed over to get a closer look.

"Yeah, Tom has some interesting things in here."

"What's that?" I ask spotting a small round antenna-looking thing attached to some earphones.

"Those are amplifiers. Kind of like a telescope for your ears," Sandy says flatly, seemingly bored with all these contraptions.

"Why don't they just bug the place?" Mark asks.

"They sweep for bugs; besides, we wouldn't want to give them a heads up that anyone's watching."

"Right," Mark says seemingly impressed.

"But we have been able to alter their acoustical jammers and loop into their security feeds."

I walk over to the scope to get a look. Looking through

it, I blink as my eyes adjust. I can see a huge executive office with a large black desk and two black leather chairs positioned in front of it.

As I try to focus my gaze on the other things around the room, a person moves into view. It takes me a minute to realize who I'm looking at, to comprehend who the woman is. Then it hits me, it's Irina von Hilton herself. I look up and gasp.

"What is it?" Mark asks heading over to the scope.

I stand back and let him take a look.

"It's the large window on the top floor," I say after realizing that I must have jerked the scope in my shock.

"Are you talking about the brunette in the suit?"

"Yes, her. She's head of the Order. The one responsible for ... well everything."

He looks at me incredulously, then bends down to get a better look.

Gio abruptly leaves the room, Sandy staring after her.

"I still can't believe all this time they were in the top of the Pym Tower," I say somewhat accusingly to Sandy.

He sighs before saying, "Tom's been gathering info from them for a while about the meteorite."

"What does he know?"

"I honestly don't know."

"Does it have anything to do with the experiments they're doing over there?"

"All I can tell you is they've been trying to duplicate and even enhance the power the meteorite was emitting ... the power that feeds our abilities. The one that you came into contact with in the cave."

I did more than come into contact with it.

"The other thing they have been trying to figure out is ... you. Your scope of control over all of us. What you're capable of. What—"

"What I am," I say flatly.

"Jo, I know exactly what you are … you're our future," he says matter-of-factly, and for a second I almost believe him.

"So are they doing all these things in that building over there," I ask sounding almost astounded to even presume it.

"Other than Irina's executive suite, the entire top floor of the tower is where the labs are. The other two floors are the actual businesses that bring in revenue with some security mixed in."

"What about Mitchell and his crazy ops guys?"

"Irina uses Mitchell and his team to do all her manual labor, so to speak. She pays the bills, buys his toys, and he takes care of her issues. But the truth is, he's becoming a pretty big issue himself. Tom thinks he's been lying to her."

I glance over when I hear Mark make a strange noise. He's standing beside the telescope with a look of utter disbelief.

"What is it?"

He bends down to take another look. After a minute, he stands up, and now his look of astonishment is morphing into one of pure rage.

I go over to the scope and take a look. There's nothing there but the wall so I start to maneuver it around until Irina comes into view again. This can't be why he's so mad. Does he know her?

That's when she steps to the side just enough for me to see that there's someone else in the office with her. A man in a lab coat.

"Who's the man with her?" I ask, watching Mark go through an array of emotions right before my eyes. "Mark, who is it?"

"It's my father."

All I can do is stand there, mouth agape as the words sink in. Sandy heads to the scope.

After a moment Sandy says, "I recognize him. He's some

sort of meteorite expert. He's one of the most important scientists over there."

Mark looks like he's going to be sick. I grab his arm.

"Come sit down."

Looking right through me for a second, I can see him contemplating exactly how he's going to proceed next. He shakes my hand off and heads to the bedroom like a man on a mission. Gio comes out then with a puzzled look on her face.

"What's wrong with him?" she asks seemingly actually concerned. Now that's a new emotion for her.

Sandy heads into the bedroom.

Oh god, I think, realizing the direction everything is moving in. I head to the room myself, but Gio reaches out to stop me. Is she kidding? I shake her off.

"Stop and think for a second. What are you going to do, just barge in there and—"

"This has nothing to do with you, so stay out of it," Mark says to Sandy as he starts putting his bloody shirt back on.

"Not me, but what about Jo?"

"What about Jo?"

"Like you said before, she's not going to let you just go over there alone. So you're willing to put her in danger?"

Mark steps toward Sandy threateningly. "Don't you dare—"

"Guys ... please," I say stepping in between them.

Mark, acknowledging my tone, steps back.

"Jo knows I'd never do anything to hurt her. She also knows my history and understands why confronting this bastard is something I have to do," Mark says and then begins to look around the room. Is he looking for a weapon?

"I get it, I really do," Sandy shoots back.

Mark stops his searching and faces Sandy. "No, you don't. Don't stand here pretending like you know what it's like to watch helpless as your mom suffers. Suffers every god damn day, because the man she loves just took off. Just like that. Trying to explain to her youngest boy every night before bed for an entire year why it wasn't his fault that his dad didn't stick around."

Pain flashes across his face at the memory.

In a calm, pragmatic tone, Sandy says, "Listen ... I didn't mean to insinuate that I knew what you were going through. I mean, I don't ... but you have to think about this. Your dad's not some random guy. To bust into the lab—"

Gio chimes in, "It may not be as hard as you think."

We all look at her then.

"Like I told Sandy earlier, I had help escaping that lab," she says, her eyes narrowing as she seems to get lost in thought for a moment.

I can remember hearing about the testing there. The testing on others like us. By the look on her face, I can only assume she saw some of it for herself.

"So this person can help me get in there?" Mark asks breaking her moment of reflection.

I watch as her eyes rake up and down Mark's large frame. "Possibly," she says, her voice softening as her gaze lingers on his face.

"Ok, well, get 'em on the phone or whatever," Mark says looking right through her, oblivious to anything else other than his own thoughts at the moment.

"Let's think about this for a moment," Sandy interjects. "Gio, you got out, yes, but that black car showing up when it did makes me wonder."

"So you think I was manipulated," she scoffs, her dark eyes challenging Sandy.

It's something in the way he looks at her then that seems to shift her attitude toward him immediately.

She smirks. "I remember when you used to trust my instincts completely," she says and looks my way.

"So can you help me get in there or not?" Mark asks Gio.

Staring at him, she seems torn. What's her deal with Mark anyway? She's always used him to mess with me, to get under my skin by reminding me how desirable she can be to just about any guy. Even guys in love with someone else.

"I can and will," she says looking at him in a way that's bugging me now on a whole new level.

"But...," she says, "Sandy's right, it's too risky. The best thing for us to do right now is get to Tom. He'll be able to give us more answers and at the same time protect our little Josephine."

Obnoxious, I think, then happily remember the discs blasting into her forehead.

Sandy gets on his phone and walks out of the room. A moment later and I hear him talking to Tom. I'd know that distinctively eloquent way of speaking anywhere. A moment later and Sandy walks back in.

"Gio's right," he says. "I guess this place isn't as safe as we thought."

Gio smiles smugly not seemingly surprised at all. What's she thinking, I wonder then quickly change my mind. I don't suppose I ever want to know what she's thinking.

"Ok, then," Gio says springing into action. She goes over to the closet and pulls out some polyester brown work shirts. She holds one up next to Mark.

"This might fit a little snug on you," she says eyeing him in a way that makes me want to fling her across the room.

"What are these for?" Mark asks looking slightly uncomfortable with her gaze.

"To help get us into the building without being noticed," Sandy says.

I take a closer look at one of the shirts. Embroidered across the top of a front left pocket are the words The Ellipse Group. What does that mean?

"It's the Circle's front. It gives them access to the entire building."

I hold the shirt up as Gio smirks. Embroidered across the entire back of it are the words Dealing with scum is what we do best.

Then I get it, it's some kind of sanitation company. That's perfect, I mean who ever pays attention to the people hired to come in and clean?

"I take it the scum is The Order?"

"Yeah, another of Tom's little jokes," Gio says.

"Tom started the company years ago as a way to access some of the major buildings in the city. It's a huge operation that helps keep the Circle's eyes and ears open. I honestly don't know how it all works; only Tom knows that," Sandy says.

Ellipse is a warped circle. Clever. How is it possible that Tom, the weirdo guy that looked like a lumberjack, could be the mastermind behind all this? I would never have thought him capable in a million years.

I don on the shirt over my own and the matching hat. I'm wondering how completely stupid I look when I glance over at Mark. He looks ridiculous as he struggles to close the front snaps on a shirt so tight it looks as though it will surely rip down the seams if he so much as raises his arms.

Sandy begins to go over the logistics of how we are to separate before meeting up in a waiting garbage truck. Gross.

"There are security cameras everywhere, so keep up the act until you're inside the truck." Sandy glances at me. "Jo, you're going to need to keep your eyes down."

Everyone's silent for a moment and I know what they're thinking. It doesn't matter what we dress up as, if I make eye contact with someone or heaven forbid look directly at a camera...

"What about that crazy person in the tricked-out car?" I ask.

"We'll deal with him when we need to," Sandy says. He puts his hand on my shoulder as he walks past me.

Mark somehow manages to snap the very last button and we head for the door. Before we leave, Sandy hands us our props to complete the look and smiles at Mark.

"Sorry, big guy," he says before opening a large utility closet on the side of the kitchen and pushing one of those rolling garbage cans his way. It's completely authentic, down to the splattered goo down the side to the revolting smell.

"This will help you, well, smell the part."

7

—

Floor 12.

Pym Tower has always been the epitome of a state-of-the-art business tower. The largest in the city, I remember reading in the paper. The Pym Tower stands alone in architectural wonderment and flawless design.

I guess whoever wrote that never saw floor 12. As the elevator doors open, the first thing I notice is the chintziness. A cheap-looking mirror hangs on the wall adorned with two large houseplants on either side. I take the hallway left and after turning a corner find myself in a small lobby. Positioned off to the side is a reception desk with the most unassuming woman I've ever seen seated behind it. On the wall directly behind her are the words Dealing with scum is what we do best in black block letters. Tom really has a knack for being subtle.

With her eyes locked on her computer screen, she never even glances my way as I do what Sandy instructed and take a seat. It looks like I'm the first one here. The plan was to meet up in the twelfth-floor lobby. I only wait a minute and then Mark walks in pushing his garbage can. I would normally laugh at the sight of him looking like this, but I can't. I'm too relieved to see him.

Throwing my arms around his neck I whisper, "Thank god."

He smiles down at me then begins to looks around. The receptionist continues to stare straight ahead at her monitor. It's strange.

Sandy appears behind her all of a sudden, dressed again in normal clothes, motioning for us to follow him. He was already here? We walk right past Ms. Observant and follow him down another hallway to the right.

Entering a room at the end of the hall, I'm taken off guard when someone suddenly flings themselves at me. Ava.

"Jo! Jo! It's really you!"

"Yes," I say laughing as she hugs me.

"I knew Sandy would find you, just knew it. Tom said he wouldn't give up until he did, and here you are," she exclaims giddily, her silky blond hair pulled back away from her youthful face.

"I've been with Tom this whole time. He's so sweet, just the sweetest," she says grinning up at me before spotting Sandy across the room and heading toward him.

As I watch her throw her arms around Sandy's neck, I smile at the thought that not only is she safe, but she hasn't changed a bit. Now what she said about Tom being the sweetest, I find hard to believe.

Glancing around, I notice the room looks like any other office. Desks and filing cabinets off to the side with posters on the walls pronouncing the latest in waste management regulations. The final touch being three large recycling containers.

"Jo, Tom wants to talk to you for a moment," Sandy says gesturing toward one of the doors at the back of the room.

Hesitantly, I walk in the room and am surprised at how different it is compared to the businesslike interior of what I've seen of floor twelve so far. It's as if I've stepped into someone's modestly furnished home.

The door opens and Tom comes in, followed by Sandy.

"So a few things have changed since our last visit," Tom says eyeing me strangely. Why do I always get the feeling he's boring into my very soul when he looks at me? "You look good, healthy."

Wondering how else I should be looking right now, I just nod.

"So you ready to play this game?"

"Game?"

Sandy chimes in, "Tom..."

"Ok, ok," he says and pauses for only a second before continuing as if unable to control himself.

"Give me blow by blow of what exactly happened when you came into contact with the meteorite."

"Uh..."

"And just keep in mind that whatever you think I don't know about that thing sitting up there in the mountain, I do. Now, go ahead tell me what happened."

"I, um..." My mind goes blank under his scrutiny.

"So the meteorite took away your ability to think," he says with a straight face.

Sandy clears his throat and says, "Tom, listen, you don't have to be this way. You can trust her."

"I'll decide when and who to trust."

Turning back to me, he sighs, then says, "Listen, I saw you outside the cave. I saw what you were capable of. Before you went in and when you came out. Cool shit, by the way. We all move fast, sure, but you ... man, you were unbelievable."

I just stare.

"I'm impressed, but I have a feeling that's just the tip of the iceberg. That's why I want to help you."

"Help me then," I say and give him a skeptical look.

His eyes seem to light up. "Tell me what happened."

What is it with this guy? What does he want from me? I already feel violated enough by the fact that he was watching me on the mountain. Then it hits me...

"But if you saw me, then you saw..."

He saw me suffering and didn't do anything to help. Who does that?

He then does something I've never seen him do before— he thinks before he talks.

"Jo, I know what you're thinking. You see, I don't ... can't trust you yet, no matter what Sandy says. I respect the guy more than anyone I've ever known, and that's saying a lot, but I gotta find out about you myself. It's just the way I work. You aren't an Ava ... someone I can read right away. Someone pure of mind and spirit. No, you're different ... complicated. From what I've seen, mostly dangerous, I just don't know how yet."

He's right. He's completely right. And as he stares at me, contemplating me, he sees it coming before I even know what I'm doing.

I've reached out and grabbed his arm. My hand against his chest, he begins to scream. I look at Sandy and want him to hit the ground. He does with a thud. Then a blinding flash.

A minute later and I loosen my grip on his arm. Tom flies back against the wall as I pull my hand away from his chest. I had another vision. A different one this time.

Suddenly the door blows open and Gio runs in the room. She stops short and I can tell she's trying to figure out what the hell is going on. Mark and Ava rush in right behind.

Tom's lying on the floor groaning, grabbing at his chest as if to stop the burning.

Oh god, not again, I think and run over to him, half-expecting him to either recoil or maybe even hit me. Instead he grabs my arm.

He's about to say something, but as he looks deep into my eyes, he freezes. I realize he's watching my eyes do their bizarre move thing. Not just the crazy-looking unearthly black pattern that's suddenly appeared within the strange amber color of my eyes, but the way they seem to look right at him while also glancing around the room. I know it's happening ... I not only feel it, I see it.

I slam my eyes closed. When I look down at him again, he's smiling at me, actually smiling as if he's excited or something. God, he is strange!

"Your eyes ... that's incredible," Tom says seemingly unable to stop staring.

I never would have thought someone could ever be so astounded by my alien eyes.

Gasping for breath, he heaves, "Did ... did you see it? The ... the vision? You were in that place ... with the light. You were..."

I nod. So he saw it, too? The vision? The same thing I did?

"God damn, did you see it too?" he asks Sandy.

Sandy's sitting up, looking as if he's trying to recover from having the wind knocked out of him. He shakes his head.

"So just the two of us then. Linked in some sort of..." I can see Tom working it through in his mind. "Did you feel what I felt?" he asks.

The vision is vivid. He was proud of me, and it made me ... happy.

"I did."

He gets up and begins to mutter to himself excitedly as I glance over at Sandy. I know what he's thinking because I'm thinking it, too. The vision was more than some loony daydream that popped into our head during a moment of ... what? What exactly is happening between us?

"Holy shit!"

Tom's rubbing his hand over his chest and there, freshly branded right above his heart, is a symbol. Not like mine or Sandy's, but one of the other ones. One of the twelve.

Tom abruptly leaves the room with Ava right behind.

"Jo, are you all right?" Mark comes over and takes my hand, squeezing it reassuringly.

I look over at Sandy, who's sitting up taking it all in. Our eyes lock and I realize he's thinking what I'm thinking. We each saw a vision the night he got his symbol. The same vision.

A few seconds later, Tom runs back in the room. I've never seen him like this before, so excited. He goes over to a small wooden table in the pseudo kitchen area and sets down some papers. Rubbing his fingers over the raised flesh where his new brand is, he mutters, "I'm a part of this then."

A part of what?

He starts looking through the papers.

"So this symbol, the one branded on me, is one of the twelve," he says, thinking more out loud than actually talking to any one of us. "Why this one, though? Why me?"

I can see him mulling it over, trying to make sense of it all.

"Jo, when you were near the meteorite did it react in some way to your presence?"

"It glowed."

"Glowed? Same as your eyes? As you were glowing in the vision?"

"Yeah, just like that."

He just stares out, thinking.

"Also, uh ... when I touched it, one of the symbols was branded on me too." I pull my shirt down to show him. Mark's eyes widen as he stares at the raised symbol burned on my flesh.

Tom comes over to get a closer look. "Holy shit, so you are connected to it. This is getting very interesting."

"Interesting, my ass. Oh my god, Jo," Mark says, and I can't tell if he's hurt because I didn't tell him or because he's getting a glimpse of what I went through while I was up on that mountain.

Ignoring Mark and continuing with his Sherlock Holmes type inquisition, "So obviously one has to be a person like us to be branded. I mean a regular person couldn't take that kind of internal heat. Our healing abilities kick in. But even so, why did you only brand me, I wonder."

"She didn't," Sandy says all of a sudden.

Tom whips around towards him.

"She branded me last night with this one," Sandy says and shows Tom the symbol I burned into his flesh.

I don't look at Mark. I don't have to, to know what he's probably thinking right now. How am I going to explain?

Tom stands there silent. Then in a whisper, he asks, "Did either of you have visions when this happened?"

We don't speak, just nod in unison. Mark storms out with Gio right behind.

"Whoa, this is some deep shit." Tom looks directly at me as he continues thinking out loud. "Weird, very weird. Visions could be what ... premonitions maybe?" I can see his mind already formulating some hypotheses as he walks back to the table and starts leafing through the papers.

"There are twelve symbols in all, and we've got three of them. So does that mean you'll be branding nine more lucky individuals?" he asks to no one in particular.

At this point, I really don't care about all this body mutilation and psycho vision crap, I just need to talk with Mark and try to explain myself. I glance at Sandy and can tell he knows what I'm thinking. We both head out of the room. I can hear Tom still throwing his questions out as we leave.

Mark and Gio aren't in the other room. Great. She probably took him somewhere to help him feel better ... her way. I groan inwardly at the thought.

As if on cue she strolls in the room.

"Where's Mark?" I ask.

She smiles and it seems genuine. My god, she's good.

"Don't worry, Josephine. I talked with him. Reminded him about how different and of course special you are. How much you care about him."

"You did, huh. Well, where is he? I'd like to talk with him myself." I give her a snide look.

"He's in the men's restroom."

I walk past her.

"Jo, it's the other way," Sandy says coming up behind me. He reaches out and grabs my arm.

"Jo, about that vision we had."

"Sandy, I really don't want to talk about that right now. Especially, right now."

"I know, I'm sorry. I just don't want you worrying about it or—"

Gio then peers her head out of the door and exclaims, "Tom needs you both to get in here right now ... Mark has left floor twelve."

8

—

Sandy and I follow Gio to another room off of the main one. Some sort of place used for surveillance, full of monitors and camera equipment.

"That stupid oaf," Tom shouts at one of the screens. Seated quietly in front of him is a tall, slim techie with glasses who appears to be in his late twenties. He looks familiar, but I can't place him.

I move up to get a look at the screen. On it, I see Mark in the stairwell running up the stairs like a man on a mission. I immediately know where he's headed.

"He's going after his father," I practically yell.

"God damn, it's too soon," Tom says staring intently at the monitor in front of him.

"What do you mean, too soon?" Sandy asks with an edge to his voice.

"We have no choice ... start it," Tom says to the tech guy, ignoring Sandy's question.

"Start what? Tom, what the hell is going on?" Sandy asks louder this time.

"This whole damn thing's in jeopardy because you two can't—" he stops himself suddenly and looks away from Sandy. "Oh, screw it."

"They're almost in position," the guy says in a serious tone, staring pensively at one of the screens.

Who's almost in position?

Halfway up a stairwell, Mark stops to rest. He grabs at his side, and that's when I've seen enough. I'm not going to wait around for Tom to use Mark in one of his cockamamie plans. I've got to help Mark.

I turn to go.

"Jo, hang on!" Sandy says, blocking my way.

"Sandy, move!"

"Just let him go; we'll get him back. Stay here, Jo. Stay safe," he says, almost pleading.

"We have him," Tom yells.

Relief surges through me as I go back in to see for myself.

Sure enough, three men are escorting Mark to an elevator. My pulse quickens as I watch Mark struggle to even walk. The stairs must have really taken it out of him.

"What about the towers' security cameras?" Sandy asks. Anyone would notice that something's off with these four.

"I've already started a feed loop. We're the only ones watching real-time data," the man sitting in the chair says glancing at me reassuringly. "Another perk of having access to every room with a garbage pail in it."

That's when I recognize him. He's the elevator guy, the one who gave me the key to Sandy's loft. Tom knew we would be there, but how? It must have been Gio. He had a hand in rescuing her and with her text to Sandy to meet there. I shake my head as all the little coincidences over the last couple of hours start to add up. Somehow Tom planned all this. No wonder he's pissed that Mark's thrown a wrench in things.

We all watch as Mark and one of the men get on the elevator. Before the other two have a chance to step on, a woman dressed in a fancy suit and heels runs down the hall asking them to please hold the elevator for her. This distraction gives Mark a split-second opportunity, which he takes. He uses his massive frame to push the one guy out of the elevator into the other two. The doors to the elevator slide close.

Tom swears and I take off.

"Jo," I hear Sandy yell as I bolt out of the room and down the hall toward the elevator. The receptionist isn't at her desk, and I realize that's probably how Mark was able to leave in the first place. I curse her work ethic as I dash by the desk and around the corner. I push the button to the elevator just as Sandy comes into the lobby.

"Wait! Jo ... wait!"

Ignoring him, I see a door at the very end of the hall with an exit sign illuminated above it—the stairs.

I'm through the door and heading the twenty-eight floors to the top. I push myself to move faster, to get to the top ... now. The expectations of my own abilities are accurate and I'm there, busting through the door sooner than I should be.

I come through the emergency exit at the end of a short hall. Even as I speed down the hall and around the corner, I notice the extravagance of this floor.

I whoosh over to the receptionist desk and almost trip over a guy sprawled out on the floor. Mark's been here. It's only a second and I have him in my sights. He's halfway down the hall leaning against the wall grasping his side.

The next second I'm behind him, reaching for him. Sensing someone, he swings at me but I easily avoid his giant arm and come around to face him.

"Jo?"

"Mark," I whisper as my subconscious suddenly realizes where we are. We're in the lion's den now.

"You shouldn't be here," he says ignoring my concern. "You need to go."

I feel the air shift and Sandy runs up, out of breath and looking pissed. He glares at Mark then abruptly looks down the hall just as I hear it, too. Voices coming from around the corner, but getting closer.

"We better get the hell out of here," Sandy says through clenched teeth.

"Yes, that's exactly what the two of you need to do," Mark says matter-of-factly, eyeing Sandy then turning to walk off.

"Mark," I say pleading. He's bleeding through his shirt.

I spot a closed door a few feet down the hall to the right. For all I know, Mitchell could be on the other side of it. Sitting there sharpening his knives, plotting his next move in his quest to end my life. But with the voices coming up fast I don't have time to second-guess my only option. Running past Mark, I get to the door and turn the knob. It's open, and the room is empty.

"Mark, please."

He seems torn but ducks into the room. I follow him in with Sandy gently closing the door behind us just as the voices come around the corner. Holding my breath, I realize they could be coming in here. We seem to be in some sort of computer storage room.

The people continue past our door. I'm relieved but then I look at Mark and Sandy. They're glaring at each other.

"Mark, why did you just take off like that?" I ask.

He seems unsure for a moment as his eyes linger on mine, but then he glances over at Sandy and his jaw clenches. "Listen Jo, I'm going to leave this room and do something I've wanted to do for a very long time. You guys should get out of here."

"I'm not leaving you," I say glancing down at his blood-stained shirt. "I'm not leaving you to face him alone."

His eyes soften even as he tests my resolve. "That's exactly what you're going to do. Honestly Jo, this has nothing to do with any of you."

His words sting but I push it away. "How can you say that? We are all involved in this."

He glances from me to Sandy as his unspoken words pierce my heart. So this has something to do with what he heard downstairs.

Guilt-ridden, the words start to flow. "I'm sorry, I know I should have told you about what happened—about the symbols. It's just I honestly didn't know what happened. It was all so strange. I mean one minute we're just standing there, then ... well—"

"Jo, this really isn't about that."

"How can it not be, I mean ... you just left and I–"

"You know, I'm not mad that the two of you had some kind of bonding moment or whatever," Mark says abruptly. "It's just that you kept me in the dark, Jo. You made me feel like an asshole, like some dumb schlep who—"

Suddenly, some of the machines start beeping just as some random light above the door begins to flash. Footsteps tromp down the hall, and Sandy pushes me toward Mark while he grabs the doorknob.

"Don't open it," I whisper intently, hoping he's not thinking of doing anything heroic.

He puts his fingers to his lips and waits. The footsteps fade.

"We better get out of here. Mark, I'll head out first while you bring up the rear," Sandy whispers then hurriedly opens the door. After checking to make sure we're alone in the hall, Sandy heads out, motioning for us to follow. I glance at Mark before heading out. I feel horrible for hurting him but know once we have a moment alone I'll be able to explain better ... to remind him that he's more important to me than any of this branding crap, hell, than anything.

Following right behind Sandy, I keep up with him easily as he moves at a brisk pace along the corridor then past the reception desk. Coming around to the elevators, I sigh with relief, seeing that the coast is shockingly clear.

Glancing back, my heart drops. Mark's gone.

Without hesitation I take off, back to the computer room. It's empty.

But I don't have the time to dwell … I have a pretty good idea where he's headed.

I make my way around the corner to another long hall. I'm half-expecting to find him here, opening every door, searching every room until he finds his dad.

My pulse jumps, reminding me how Mark has a way of shaking my sense of control. He seems to be my trigger.

The hall splits. I stand there listening for any sign of him.

That's when I hear it: "Dad." The one word that tells me it's Mark and he's found exactly who he's looking for.

From behind, someone grabs my arm and spins me around.

"Jo, wait," Sandy says out of breath, his eyes pleading.

I yank my arm out of Sandy's grasp and run in the direction of Mark's voice. I get to the end of that hall and it splits again. For god's sake, this damn labyrinth.

"Son, I'm sorry you're a part of all this," I'm able to zero in on and hear a voice say. I see two large swinging gray doors at the end of the hall. Without even the slightest hesitation, I push through the doors.

Blinking, it takes only a second for my eyes to adjust from the stark contrast of the muted lighting in the hall to this … a ceiling equipped with hundreds of recessed lights, flooding the room in ultra bright light.

Sandy bursts into the room behind me and pauses to take it all in.

Gleaming stainless-steel machinery of various shapes and sizes rests atop a massive white table positioned directly in the center of the room. Just past the impressive table are other rooms sectioned off by glass walls and doors. These rooms seem to house laboratory equipment, like you'd expect to see inside some high-tech research facility.

It's then that I notice all the bodies. Men and women, dressed in white lab coats, sprawled out on the floor of the lab.

"It's you."

I look up and find Mark gaping at me. Not Mark himself, but an older version of him.

"I'm Gregor," Mark's father says, holding his hand out to me, smiling in amazement as he stares at my eyes as if they aren't even a part of me.

"Keep her out of this," Mark says angrily glaring at him.

"Mark, we can't," a voice says suddenly from the side of the room. It's his younger brother Harrison. A slightly smaller version of Mark but with the light-green eyes of his mother.

Mark and I stand there shocked. What is he doing here? Harrison walks toward me.

Sandy's there in a second, shoving him away from me. He lands on the floor but quickly gets up. Gio bursts into the lab. She leaps past me and kicks Sandy in the chest, sending him sailing across the room. Before I have time to think about what he's doing, Harrison grabs my hand and shoves it onto his chest.

I'm unable to move as Gregor grabs for Mark and Harrison screams. Then the flash.

A shudder runs through my body but he urges me on. "Trust me, Jo," I hear him say, and I do. I do with all my being. Through the darkness he pulls me, his firm grip on my hand never slackening.

She laughs and I turn. I'm on a stony ledge that I've seen before. Ava twirls all around a smiling Harrison, her white dress billowing out around her. I can't help but laugh as I watch the spectacle before me.

He reaches his hand out to me, and I take it without hesitation. I follow his gaze until it rests on the horizon. There are two suns, one slightly smaller than the other. That's when I hear the cheering ... then my name.

"Jo!"

Looking in the direction of the voice I see Mark, struggling to get out of his father's grasp. My mind connects and Harrison goes flying to the floor.

"Sandy, I had to." Gio says apologetically to Sandy just as Gregor, releasing his hold on Mark, runs over to Harrison. Harrison's trying to catch his breath and sit up all the while staring at me.

"Son, are you all right?"

He nods and slowly gets to his feet with Gregor's help.

Gregor reaches over and pulls Harrison's shirt down to reveal a branded symbol. "My god, you were right," he says to Harrison.

Sandy grabs my arm. "Jo, are—"

"I'm fine," I say, knowing the look.

"Jo," I hear Harrison say. "Jo, can you hear me?"

What the hell. Harrison's talking to me without speaking out loud.

"I know you hear me," he says.

"Jo, it's very important that you trust in the visions. Trust in the way they make you feel as much and maybe even more than what you see."

I look between Mark and Sandy.

"Can you hear him, too ... in your head?" I ask the two of them.

They both give me an odd look. Mark takes it a step further.

"What the hell is going on?" he asks loudly.

"The power source," Gregor says suddenly to nobody in particular and heads over to a large metal contraption in the back of the room.

Harrison's like a boy on a mission. As he looks at Mark now, his perspective seems to change.

Eyes pleading for him to understand, Harrison says, "Mark, I've been having visions, well ... more than that. I've..."

As he struggles to find the right words, Gio chimes in.

"Mark, your little brother is one of us."

"One of you?"

"Yes. It seems that when Josephine was in the cave—changing, or whatever she was doing in there—Harrison came into his abilities. You should have heard the things your brother has told me."

Mark, having a hard time comprehending what Gio's saying, stares at Harrison in disbelief as he murmurs, "You're one of them?"

"Yes, he is, and I have to say ... he's pretty amazing," Gio says and winks at Harrison, causing him to instantly blush.

"Harrison, but how..." Mark can't seem to bring himself to ask as he stares at his brother.

"Not just me ... dad, too," Harrison says, his eyes pleading for Mark to understand.

"Dad?"

I watch as he struggles to grasp it all.

"You see, I knew Jo would brand me with this symbol," Harrison says matter-of-factly. "That part of the vision was clear."

Gregor pulls a lever, and the platform that the huge metal cylinder is resting on begins to rise. At the same time, the ceiling starts to open up revealing a star-filled sky.

"Jo, that's the machine my dad has been working on. Someone is coming. Someone very important," Harrison says again without moving his mouth.

"Who's coming?" I ask, and everyone else looks at me as

if I've lost my mind.

"I don't have time to explain," he says. "Please, just trust me to do what I say."

Instantly, his words touch on something deep within me and I do, I trust him completely.

"She isn't trusting anyone until I find out what's going on," Mark says glancing towards Gregor.

Tom storms in with Ava right behind. "Whoa ... Gregor, good job taking out the probers," Tom says, seemingly impressed as he looks at the bodies scattered about.

"Yes, well, I had no other choice since you changed the time–"

"Are they dead?" Gio asks suddenly looking around with a sense of smug satisfaction.

Gregor exclaims, "Goodness no! They're just anesthetized. It's my own concoction using a system of expressed air and—"

"Harrison, you got your badge of honor," Tom asks and moves to get a closer look. "I'll be damned ... it's another of the twelve!"

"It's exactly the same symbol I saw in my vision," Harrison says.

"Is that right? Well, your vision failed to tell me I was gonna get one of my own," Tom says and grins as he shows Harrison his newfound pride and joy.

"Tom, what the hell's going on?" Sandy asks angrily.

Ava runs over to Harrison and grabs the front of his shirt as she smiles sweetly at Sandy.

"Sandy, don't worry. Harrison knows about things before they happen, and he says I'm gonna get a symbol of my very own," she says and gently grazes her fingers over Harrison's brand. He seems frozen, captivated by her touch. I watch their interaction bemused until suddenly it hits me and I realize what she just said.

Wait ... what! What's she talking about? Instantly I feel panicky and hold my hand out in front of me as I back away from them. I know it seems like everyone that's gotten one of these crazy brands are alright, still alive and kicking, but I don't know what it really means to get one. What if it ends up being some crazy mark that somewhere down the road leads to our demise. I can't let Ava become a part of all this, not when we don't know what this is.

"Stay away from me," I say hearing the alarm in my own voice.

"Jo, it's all right. This is the way it's supposed to happen," Harrison says without moving his mouth again.

"And you, stay out of my head!"

"All right, let's just calm down," Tom says looking at Sandy and me. "Everyone that's conscious in the room right now is on the same side, wants the same things. So let's just take a deep breath and get some perspective here."

Just then others run in. One's the tech guy from downstairs followed by the three men from the elevator and the slack receptionist.

"Sandy," Tom says. "You know me. Until recently, the only thing I gave a rat's ass about was taking down this, pain in my ass, organization."

Sandy nods.

Smiling at Harrison, he goes on, "But things have changed. You see, Harrison here has recently come into his powers. He's become some sort of cool-ass psychic or something and according to him, there's a ... well, you could call it a prophecy of sorts," he says then shrugs as if he knows it all sounds loony.

"Prophecy?" I ask, suddenly feeling like I'm being punk'd. If it weren't for everything I've been through, I'd probably start laughing at the insanity of it all.

"His word, not mine. But one that's going to change all our lives," Tom says more matter-of-factly this time.

Hurriedly, the tech guy interrupts, "Tom, just as you thought, Mitchell detected the machine. He's headed to the meteorite."

"Shit. Gregor, you have your device in place out there and ready to go?"

"Yes hypothetically, but again, it's never been tested."

"Well shit, let's hope it works. Mitchell needs to be good and knocked out when Gio gets there."

Turning his attention back to the first guy, he asks, "And the virus?"

"It's ready, even on all the backup systems. Once it's implemented, there won't be any trace. Just the usual fat-cat corporate trail."

"Perfect."

"Remember, even after they're gone, we have to wait until the machine cycles completely through before starting the virus," Gregor says loudly as he begins gathering up some sort of extension cord.

"Don't forget about this one," Gio says disdainfully, using her shoe to nudge the head of a redheaded woman lying on the floor.

"Just put her in the same car as before," Tom says to Ava, and she walks over to the woman and puts her hand on her chest. She instantly disappears.

Gio gives a look of satisfaction and smirks at Tom. "Perfect. Now we'll go and run your little errand then take care of Mitchell," she says and motions to the receptionist lady and three men to follow her, tossing her glistening hair back as she bounds out the door, the others right behind.

Tom watches them leave as if deep in thought. What

errand? And what same car as before? I could swear he seems torn about something, which gives me a bad feeling.

The machine begins to make a loud whirring noise. Everyone's breath catches as they stop and stare.

Tom, instantly recovered from his moment of reflection, exclaims in a loud voice, "Harrison, I sure hope you're right about this!"

Harrison just smiles and turns to Ava and nods. Ava goes up to Mark and says sweetly, "Time to send you someplace safe. Better hold your breath." Then she quickly places her hand on his chest and he's gone.

9

—

Sandy grabs my arm as my knees begin to buckle. Things are moving too fast. The semblance of control that I felt even a moment ago is gone.

"Where did you send him?" I ask Ava, my voice shaky.

"Oh Jo, don't worry. He's safe at that warehouse place," Ava says smiling at me as if there's nothing to worry about.

"Warehouse ... but where..."

My pulse quickens.

Seeing Gregor head toward me with those extension cord things, Sandy places himself between me and everyone else in the room. Gregor stops, suddenly comprehending Sandy's apprehension.

"She has to be connected to the replicate power source to be able exponentially increase the meteorites' output enough to open the portal," he says in an oddly pragmatic tone.

Rolling his eyes. "For god sakes Gregor," Tom says irritatingly. "Jo, someone very important needs to come through that meteorite of yours, and the only way to do that is to wake the sucker up. So per Harrison here, we need to juice you up by connecting you to that machine, then send you into the cave so you can do your thing ... whatever the hell that is."

"It's reaching maximum output now," Gregor says hurriedly as the metal contraption gets louder by the second.

"Tom, you can't possibly be serious! Putting her life in danger to—"

"Sandy, this is exactly why I kept you in the dark. It

seems lately your only goddamn concern is..."

He catches himself even though everyone knows what he was going to say.

"Tom, we need to do this now," Gregor says eyeing him.

Tom swings at Sandy in an attempt to knock him away from me. Sandy easily dodges the strike then backhands him, sending him to the ground.

"Jo, trust me," Harrison says and reaches for my hand.

Trust him? This is all so crazy, too crazy, I think as I stare at Harrison. Trust Mark's younger brother...

"No, it's all right," I say to Sandy, wondering why it suddenly feels right to do exactly what Harrison needs me to.

Harrison takes my hand then motions Ava over. "You must focus your thoughts on the cave ... on the meteorite. Think back on your time there. I really can't explain it, but you have to feel it," Harrison says.

"Ava can only transport someone to a place she's been. So the only way she can take you to the meteorite is if she's able to go into your thoughts and feel the location for herself. Make your memories her own. This is where I come in. I'll try controlling the vision while guiding your memories and feelings of the cave into her own thoughts. But Jo, you have to focus, no matter how much, uh ... you're distracted, while she's being branded."

"What! I'm not branding her," I say and pull my hand away.

"Jo, for whatever reason you choose her. She's meant to be a part of this and in a minute when you're connected to her, you brand her. I saw it."

"I don't care what you saw. I'm not choosing her, I'm not consciously choosing anyone."

"Somewhere deep down you are. You're the one choosing us. Can you come here a second," he asks of the tech guy that until this point seemed to be getting a big kick out of watching our interchange.

"Me?"

"Yeah, hurry ... come here."

The guy hesitantly comes over and Harrison slams my hand against his chest.

The guy seems frozen in horror as he stands there waiting for something to happen, but nothing does.

"He's a person like us but nothing happened. You see ... you are only branding some of us. I believe the same number of symbols that I saw in my vision is the number of us that will get one of these," Harrison says and looks down at his.

"But I can't—"

Gregor pushes the guy away and connects the cord to me with some sort of adhesive strap right across my chest.

"I doubt it has to be in any particular area for you, but just in case," Gregor says then backs up as if he's waiting for me to explode or something.

I don't explode, but the look on his face tells me something is happening. A glow is beginning to radiate throughout my body.

Sandy's beside me now reaching for the strap.

"For Christ's sake," I hear Tom say.

"No, wait! She'll be all right, I promise," Harrison pleads.

I push his hand away before he's able to mess with the strap and stare up into his face, so handsome, so ... perfect, reflecting my own uncertainties back at me.

For the first time, I realize what my demise would mean for him. The gravity of this knowledge sends pangs of guilt coursing through me. I should probably reassure him, heck at the very least act grateful, but I don't.

"Ava," Harrison says.

She comes over smiling as if she's about to be crowned Miss USA.

"Remember what we talked about?"

She smiles and nods.

Harrison's in my head then. "Concentrate on the meteorite, the cave. Think back, Jo."

I hesitate.

"Jo," he yells in my head as he grabs my hand.

I take my thoughts there. I can feel my heart rate speed up as I think of myself standing back in front of that glowing rock. The same urge floods my senses and I instinctively reach out to touch it. To run my fingers over its smooth surface.

Images start to push their way in as Ava's vision surges.

Plunging the blade in fuels my fury.

I turn and with the same precision find my mark yet again. Even as the fluidity of my actions begins to tip the scales in this war, I can sense her near me … whimpering, bleeding … dying.

I hear Harrison's voice suddenly.

"Jo, concentrate on the meteorite!"

I focus my thoughts until I finally find myself exactly where I need to be.

Back in the cave … in the cave with my entire body glowing as I stand in front of this big, dark rock. It only takes me a second to shake off the lingering feelings from that last vision and remember. Remember why I'm here, what I'm supposed to do.

I shove my hand against its smooth surface and brace myself for its reaction. I don't know if I'm expecting to be thrown back or maybe even combust altogether, but I'm surprised at what happens … nothing.

I glance around, looking for guidance. There's no one. Concentrating, I hope to hear Harrison tell me what to do next.

Now what do I do? If I'm this special person, shouldn't

something just magically happen? Concentrate Jo, I tell myself knowing that this is anything but fiction.

It just pops in my head. The memory of being at that mission compound. The anguish I felt as I hovered over Ava right after I made her heart stop ... and right before I started it again. Yes, these are the feelings I need to muster up to be able to go into the depths of this bag of tricks I possess.

I take myself back and begin to feel the pain associated with the memories ... feel the emotions needed to wake up this particular ability. Tears sting my eyes as the burning sensation in the pit of my stomach starts to make its way up into my throat.

Why does this always have to be so hard?

I concentrate on what I need to do. On this energy source that is within me—hell, is me. But nothing happens. My mind suddenly switches. It goes blank just as my body responds.

"...trust in the visions. Trust in the way they make you feel..."

Harrison's words flash in my mind, and I finally start to get it. My abilities have always been connected to my emotions, but I have to feel them to control them.

And suddenly, I'm feeling them!

It's like a switch has just been turned on and I can feel the power from within me waking up ... reacting. I sense that I could be capable of so much more. Excitement courses through me. Whoa Nelly, settle down girl, and just get through this thing first, I tell myself.

The meteorite begins to glow as I push the force out through my hand. I give a slightly stronger push and watch the glow become brighter as the energy is absorbed faster, spreading through the rock. Now that's cool.

I push harder.

Suddenly, there's a whooshing noise then a flash. My eyes slam shut as I jump back away from the meteorite.

"What the hell?" I hear Tom say all of a sudden from behind me.

Glancing over, I see him, Harrison, Ava, and Sandy standing there staring at me in disbelief. All those I've branded have somehow joined me.

My eyes lock on Sandy, and I can see his relief at having me in his sights ... safe with him again.

"Now my vision makes sense," Harrison says staring at something behind me.

"Holy crap," Tom says also staring in awe.

I turn around and come face to face with a captivatingly gorgeous woman. The slender, tall figure with copper skin and fine features just stands there, eyes closed, as if in a deep meditative state. She's dressed in a white pantsuit made of a fabric I can't quite place. It's just as exotic and captivating as its wearer.

Nobody utters a sound until she suddenly opens her eyes. The others gasp as I stare in disbelief at the eyes now looking directly at me. Luscious dark waves frame the face of the only other person I've ever seen with eyes like mine. Their amber hue with the odd black pattern isn't the only similarity, it's the movement—the way they seem to have a life of their own. I was freaked out seeing it in the mirror in Sandy's cabin, but somehow watching them sporadically glance around the room while seemingly not ever having her take her eyes off me brings a new level of freak to my consciousness.

"Her eyes are like yours, Jo," Ava says curiously.

As if understanding exactly what Ava said, the woman smiles at me suddenly, a smile of acknowledgment, recognition.

Tom steps forward then. "Welcome to, uh, Earth."

Even as her head turns slightly in his direction, her eyes move by their own accord.

"I, uh ... we have been expecting you. Well, not necessarily you, I mean. We weren't sure what to expect, I mean...."

As Tom rambles, I can't help but stare. Other than the eyes, she's the most beautiful person I've ever seen. Is she a person at all? Is she even human?

"She's altered to become a manifestation of Jo's ideal human," Harrison says, then seems surprised by himself for saying it. "It's weird, that just popped in my head."

"Yes, she is beautiful," Ava says smiling at her.

The meteorite's amber glow slowly begins to fade out. I remember back to the last time its glow was extinguished. I push the memory away but still feel a dull ache in the pit of my stomach.

That's when she speaks to me.

"Be not afraid of your greatness, for it is said you were born great, will thrust greatness upon others, and will achieve greatness."

We all stand in silence. It's not just the incredibly soothing quality of her voice that's astounding, or the fact even that some out-of-this-world entity has just spoken. No, it's her actual words. Her first words were ... a misquote. A misquote of Shakespeare. Is she kidding?

Sandy leans in and whispers, "Did she just attempt to quote—"

Tom clears his throat. "Hi again, um ... Tom, I mean, I'm Tom. Just curious ... how it is that you speak English?"

She smiles at him. "Yes ... Tom," she says in such a way as to savor the very sound of his name. "I am what some would call a seer. That is how I know all your languages."

"You can speak all of them?" Tom asks in disbelief.

"Ná," she says smiling.

Tom glances at Sandy.

"It's 'yes' in your Elvish language."

"Our Elvish... Oh wow, I would say some things have been lost in translation."

Her gaze seems to bore right into Tom's very soul. She nods slightly then, as if coming to some conclusion within herself.

"Your intuition is quite remarkable. It will be a great strength to the twelve."

"The twelve ... my intuition," Tom says as if trying to wrap his head around her odd examination of him.

"But I must caution you, Tom," she says again, expressing his name in the same strange way, "be wary of your gift as it can also be a sword with two sharp sides."

"A double-edged sword?"

She just smiles.

Tom seems taken aback and speechless for the first time. Ava introduces herself next.

Her voice grows very soft as she looks at Ava. "Your likeness to your great ability is fascinating."

"I have a great ability?"

"To the twelve you will be their mucilage."

"Mucilage ... to the twelve. Well that sounds exciting," Ava says touching the front of her shirt proudly. Touching her newly acquired symbol.

Ava smiles sweetly at her. "So, what is your name? Why are you here?"

She seems to contemplate the questions for a moment then looks at me before answering, "I'm exactly what you need right now."

"Exactly what I need?" I ask.

"You may call me Guida. It's a name originating from your Italian cultures. It seems the most fitting," she says.

"Isn't that a form of Guido?" Tom says snickering to himself.

"I think it's a wonderful name," Ava says sweetly.

"The name means 'guide.' You're here to guide us, I mean to guide Jo, and us," Harrison says, seeming confused.

Guida seems baffled for a moment as she stares at Harrison. She then closes her eyes as if concentrating on something.

We've crossed so far into the world of unbelievable that I'm not surprised by anything at this point. Sandy looks at me and smiles but I see his apprehension.

Still in her deep concentrated state she says, "It is told that someone will possess within them the one true energy source. The source necessary for life."

"Necessary for life?" Tom repeats worriedly.

Opening her eyes, she looks right at me. "You are this person. You are the one that can change the future of my world and your own."

"Change the future? Uh ... I can do what?" I ask.

She smiles. "No need to question. Magnificence will come easily to you."

Easily. Oh boy, she doesn't know me.

Harrison laughs, making the others seem confused as they glance at him.

"Your connection with the true source is impressive," she says to him. "You should be cautious as no one will be closer to her than you, and without you, she shall be lost."

Harrison just stares at her. She just told a young teenage boy that not only is he going to be the closest person to some freaky cosmic hero, but to his brother's girlfriend. Talk about messed up dynamics.

Harrison turns red, and I instantly curse that damn mind reading thing.

"Everyone on my world carries with us the hope that you, and the chosen eleven, give us all the promise of a future. That is why I have come, to help guide the hope of our future."

I feel sick to my stomach.

She looks at me oddly.

"So once she's done choosing the eleven, what happens then?" Tom asks inquisitively, as if already trying to formulate a plan.

"Jo takes us to my world," she says, reaching out and gently touching the meteorite hesitantly.

"You mean ... wait ... using that," Tom asks surprisingly, then smiles at me, just a lot less assuredly this time.

"Well, we're not going anywhere in that until we figure out the best way to leave here," Sandy says glancing at the cave entrance worriedly reminding us of the one person we should be worrying about right now ... Mitchell.

Turning to Tom he asks, "In the lab you mentioned a device that's out there somewhere."

"Oh, right, the device. Yeah, I guess we can't save worlds if we don't save ourselves first," Tom says.

"So what exactly does it do?"

"It's one of Gregor's toys. I really don't know much about the science, just that it's supposed to pop out of the ground and knock out anyone that happens to be within a certain perimeter." Tom sounds less than confident.

"What's the problem?" Sandy asks suspiciously.

"Gregor was never able to test it. So if the fucker didn't work, we're sitting ducks in here if Mitchell decides to show up."

"What if I transport everyone?" Ava asks as if hoping to help diffuse the tension.

Shaking his head Tom says, "No, we're not leaving you alone."

"She won't be, I'll stay," Sandy says.

"I'm not leaving the two of you to possibly face Mitchell. No, we'll just have her transport Harrison and Guida."

"Yes, I can transport you to safety," Ava says to Guida smiling. "It's something I'm able to do."

Tom glances at Guida, "But will your mojo work on her—"

"I'm not supposed to leave that way," Harrison suddenly interjects. "I mean, I saw myself walking through the trees, walking with Jo ... unless ... it's not what happens now. I just feel..." Harrison closes his eyes as if to concentrate harder. "I don't know ... it's so fuzzy."

Tom takes what Harrison says seriously. "All right, so we know we aren't sending you and Jo over, but—"

"Not sending Jo, are you serious?" Sandy says loudly.

Guida stares at Sandy sympathetically. Why is she looking at him like that?

"You do not exaggerate Jo's importance to your existence ... Sandy," Guida says enjoying the syllables in his name more than anyone should. "Even as you feel this within your own essence, so shall she, as the two of you ... are one. This is your reality."

"Oh, oh ... I just knew it," Ava exclaims.

I stand there trying to look as if I'm deciphering her words, but they resonate within me instantly. She's telling me something I already somehow know.

"At least that explains his unreasonable need to protect her," Tom mutters out loud embarrassing me further.

I glance at Harrison. The brother to the one person I know I love, have always loved on some level. No, I can't be completely without choices in this whole thing. I refuse to be. That's when the answer pops in my mind: free will. Whatever conclusions fate has bestowed on my life, I have the ultimate veto power. I have free will.

"You're right, Jo, you'll get to make your own choices about uh … things," Harrison says, to my chagrin, out loud.

If Sandy's hurt by my thoughts, he doesn't let on.

"Yes. You're speaking of your choices … of changes to your fate. To all our fates. For this is what brought me here … the prophecy.

That word again … prophecy. I mean it all sounds so insane.

Guida gives me a strange look.

"So how do we go about testing Ava's abilities on you?" Tom says to Guida. "Can we touch you?"

We stare at him as if he's crazy.

Guida shocks us all when she walks right up to him suddenly and puts her hand on his face. "You are right to be cautious."

"Um … sure," Tom says smiling nervously as he takes a step back away from her.

Guida continues, "I find that I am not myself on this planet, so I will not always know your answers, but my purpose may be to intervene … so, your intentions are not for me."

"Okay … yeah well, we should probably keep you with us anyhow," Tom says seemingly still a little freaked out from her touch.

She nods.

Tom turns to Sandy. "Well, let's hope Gregor's toy worked. If not…"

He doesn't need to finish. We're all thinking of Mitchell and what he's capable of. Nobody knows that more than me.

"We better go," Sandy says, taking the lead but stopping when he gets close to the entrance of the cave. "Tom and I will go out first and make sure we're alone."

"Yeah, and if we aren't?" Tom mutters under his breath as he follows Sandy out.

Harrison's suddenly in my head. "Jo, I don't want to scare Ava, but for some reason I'm feeling weird about this. I keep getting hazy flashes, but nothing I can make out, at least nothing that would cause me to feel like this."

I glance over at him, but he's not even looking at me.

"Oh, and by the way, everything I see or feel is always connected to you."

Oh great, my own personal psychic.

Sandy and Tom come back telling us the coast is clear. We head out.

10

—

utside the cave's entrance, I glance over at Guida half-
expecting her to be looking around, curious about
her new surroundings. Other than some strange keen
interest in the night sky, she's not.

For a while we just walk, no one saying a word. I can see
the apprehension on Harrison and Tom's face. Ava smiles at
Harrison then grabs his hand probably hoping to set him at
ease. Ah, young love. I smile to myself thinking how cute
they look. Harrison turns bright red, and I can't help but
chuckle.

"Something funny?" Tom asks annoyed.

Ignoring him I glance over at Guida. She's hard to read
but I swear she seems to be following all our interactions,
subconscious or not, completely.

Sandy walks up beside Tom. "I want to know what your
true intention is in all this," he whispers to Tom giving me
the feeling they have been down this road before.

Tom's whole demeanor changes when he glances at Sandy.
"No, you're right, you need to know."

Tom scratches his head seemingly searching for the
words.

"The meteorite, Jo, it's all bigger than we thought. I
mean, you heard what Guida said, and I'm sorry Sandy, I
really am, but Jo's smack in the middle of it all. So you can
try to protect her, but you can't cut her out of it. You just
can't..."

"What does that have to do with you not being honest

with me about Gio, leaving me in the dark about 'your plan'," Sandy says glancing around as we all walk along but not backing down on his inquisition.

"After Gio ended up in the lab, her future as one of their lab rats was changed when Harrison showed up. Gregor was barely able get her out of there without causing suspicion."

"Why did Harrison showing up change anything?"

"Because of the things he said. We needed to get our hands on Jo and Gio knew, maybe more than anyone, that you'd never willingly get her involved in all this. Not even to bring Guida over. So Gio was our way to get to you, to ... her." Tom says motioning toward me.

Sandy's quiet as if digesting his words.

"Listen man, let's just get to the warehouse, none of that crap will matter if we don't get there. Actually we should be coming up on the perimeter soon," Tom says starting to look a little anxious.

"Wouldn't Gio have met up with us by now?" Sandy asks.

"Yeah, that's what I was thinking," Tom says then gives Sandy a look that makes my body jolt in response.

My head jerks as I see movement far up ahead to the right. Halting, I quickly try to focus.

"What is it?" Sandy asks quietly looking in the same direction.

"It's hard to tell but ... I think its smoke, or—"

"Whatever the hell it is, we're exposed right now," Tom says nervously as he glances all around.

We begin to walk tentatively closer as my eyes start to make out the object. It only takes another moment and I know exactly what I'm looking at ... a body lying on the ground, steaming.

"It's a person," I say in disbelief.

Tom runs past me, getting to the body first.

"Oh shit."

Harrison grabs Ava's arm and they halt as Guida, Sandy, and I come up on the smoldering woman. It's the lazy receptionist from earlier, the one that left with Gio. As I stare at her recently combusted body, I realize our situation has just taken a horrible turn.

"I'm thinking this can't be good," Tom says and gives Sandy a knowing look.

"The device?" Sandy asks.

"No, someone had to have done this. The device doesn't have this kind of juice."

I scan the area and listen again for any indication that we aren't alone. That's when I see another faint movement about hundred yards away. Another body.

"There's another one over there," I say pointing in its direction.

I speed over. Lying on the ground in the same condition as the woman is one of the three men that also left with Gio ... a steaming pile of what was at some point, a physically conditioned man.

I run back. "It's one of your men," I say to Tom without even a hint of breathlessness.

Sandy grabs my arm, pulling me over to Ava. "Ava, transport her to the warehouse!".

I step back away from her hand coming at me. "What ... no! I'm not leaving."

"Enough is enough, Jo. Ava," Sandy says through clenched teeth.

"Ava, don't. I'm not leaving!"

"Jo, this is Mitchell's doing! He's probably watching us right now."

Ava gasps at the mention of his name. She turns to

Harrison and before he has a chance to react, sends him away. She seems almost shocked by her instinct, but I understand ... she cares for him.

Ava shrugs. "Well, he wasn't wrong about what he saw. He did end up taking a walk with you in the woods," she says to me.

I'm actually relieved that he's gone. No matter what connection he has to me he's Mark's brother and if anything happened to him, I could never forgive myself.

"Is there cover around here besides the cave?" Sandy asks Tom.

"No," Tom says flatly. "But honestly, when it comes to Mitchell I don't think it matters much where we are. He'll get us one way or another."

Ava gasps, and Tom immediately looks sorry he said it.

"He wants me, Ava. Don't worry. So as long as I'm here, he won't hurt you," I say hoping to make Ava feel better but instead just make Sandy seemingly angrier.

"So when can we expect the reinforcements?" Sandy asks Tom sarcastically.

"Man, don't start with this shit now. You know I never leave anything to chance. But I'm the one that's supposed to be monitoring the security feeds out here while Gregor handled the virus. I didn't think I'd be actually out here in the middle of all this crap."

Tom begins to pace, thinking out loud. "Damn it. Gregor probably doesn't even know what's happened. Now with Gio and the others dead—"

"We don't know for sure that he killed Gio," Sandy says matter-of-factly.

Tom starts to say something, than changes his mind. Turning to me, he says, "Jo, now would be a really great time to tell me about your new bag of tricks."

"Tom," Sandy says threateningly.

"Fine then. Let's go," Tom says throwing his hands in the air.

As we all cautiously continue through the forest, all I can think about is how right Tom is. I am the only person here that probably has the capabilities to take on Mitchell and his cronies.

"There are two more bodies over there," I say suddenly as two distinct smoking mounds come into my line of sight.

As we all head in the direction of the corpses, I hear something like a muffled moan, coming from somewhere off in the distance. "Wait! I hear something."

Everyone stops walking and stares at me while I try to concentrate harder on the sound that's too far away for anyone else to hear. It's definitely a loan moan and . . . what? It takes my mind a minute to register the noise, but then I realize it's the faint crackling of electricity. The same sound those Taser devices make when they're frying someone, only much . . . weaker.

"This way," I say headed in its direction while feeling in my gut that something is very wrong. The crackling seems to be getting a tad louder, but I can tell no one else is hearing anything yet.

There it is again . . . a moan, and way more distinct this time.

I turn to Guida. "Can you run fast, I mean like they can?" I ask looking at the others. Although they can't run as fast as me, they are still much quicker than most.

"I can do what's intended."

Tom shrugs while I just take it upon myself to assume she means yes.

Sandy grabs my arm. "What are you hearing?"

"I'm not sure, but it sounds like someone's hurt or..."

"Let's all stay together," Sandy says flatly as he motions for me to lead the way.

I continue to hear the crackling noise getting slightly louder. A few seconds later, it stops altogether. We come up on a clearing in the trees and I stop running. We are close, I know it.

Ava's sudden intake of breath draws my attention. It takes my mind a minute to register what I'm seeing as Sandy runs ahead.

Gio, nude from the waist up, is tied against the trunk of a large tree, her head falling forward in such a way that her lustrous hair cascades down around her.

"Is she...?" Ava asks sounding shaken.

Sandy reaches out to check for a pulse when suddenly a faint moan escapes her.

"She's alive," Sandy says hurriedly as he starts to pull on the black cord that's binding her in place, digging into her flesh. As its grip on her loosens, lines of blood are left behind showing the results of such tight bondage.

The cord gives way completely, and she slumps forward into Sandy's arms.

"I got you," he says as he looks over at Tom puzzled.

I glance around the area, suddenly unsure if we are alone out here. Surely Mitchell is watching us, reveling in her misery. I don't see or hear anyone, but that doesn't convince me he's not around.

"What is it?" Sandy asks an edge to his voice.

"It's nothing. I thought maybe—"

"San...," Gio says hoarsely staring up at Sandy, pain etched all over her face.

"Hey you," Sandy says and smiles weakly down at her.

I can tell her healing abilities are beginning to kick in as I hear her breathing steady and become stronger.

"My chest..." she whispers hoarsely.

Sandy quickly gets what she's trying to say and gently places her on the ground so she's lying on her back.

"Oh shit," Tom exclaims suddenly.

Seemingly embedded within her chest cavity is some type of light source. It flickers and the crackling noise starts up again. Her body jolts in response.

"Tom, what is that thing?" Sandy asks.

As the crackling continues, Gio's breathing becomes labored as she seems to be on the brink of unconsciousness.

Tom looks at Sandy as if he doesn't want to say. "It's a device The Order was working on a while back ... an implant used for torture."

"Wha...?"

"I thought Gregor had destroyed them all," Tom says and then something seems to occur to him suddenly. "Oh shit ... that fucking redheaded bitch—"

"How do we get it out?" Sandy asks.

"You don't. These are nasty fuckers. The body heals around them. Once in place, they're remotely activated and that's ... well, when the fun begins."

"What do you mean?"

"They use the same type of energy current as those Taser things, just less of it. Basically just enough to almost kill you without pushing you over the edge."

The crackling stops and Gio moans.

I feel horrible.

"Could we cut it out of her somehow?" Sandy asks as if trying to exhaust all possibilities to save her now.

Tom shakes his head. "Gregor's gotta flip the switch on this bad boy before we try to mess with it, or it could malfunction and fry her. I've seen it happen. Fun place ... that lab."

"I can't believe Gregor would be a part of all that," I say

but then think about Mark and his issues with him.

"Hey, you can think what you want about Gregor, but if it wasn't for him, our kind would be all but wiped out," Tom says.

"So we need to get her to Gregor," Sandy says and starts to take off his shirt.

"Here, use this," Ava says handing Sandy a sweater she had on over her blouse.

"Thanks," he says and gently puts it around Gio without even a flicker of emotion. Gio moans in response and sighs shakily.

"Will transporting her trigger it?"

"That I don't know," Tom says looking down at Gio uncharacteristically concerned.

"Well, we have no choice," Sandy says matter-of-factly and picks her up in his arms to carry her.

"Wait a minute," Tom says looking around. "Sandy, this doesn't feel right. I mean, why not kill her? Why did Mitchell go through the trouble of putting that thing in her?"

He's right, I think. Mitchell doesn't do anything without a reason.

I glance around still not sensing a thing.

"Unless he's not willing to risk another tangle with Jo, especially since we've added a new member to our little entourage," Tom goes on to say.

Guida just stands there taking it all in.

"So he's not here then," Ava asks sounding hopeful.

Almost talking to himself, Tom continues. "But shit, it's Mitchell. The guy's good, hell—the best. He's probably assuming we'd be all freaked out seeing Gio like this and rush to the only person that can save her. Oh man, we'll lead him right to the one place he wants to find ... the warehouse."

"Let's head back to town. We'll figure out something when we get there," Sandy says.

We set out, moving quickly through the trees, down the mountainside. As we make headway toward our destination, the device continues through its torturous cycle on Gio. No one seems to breathe as we listen to that horrible crackling noise, knowing what it's doing to her. Once it stops and we hear a low moan, we breathe easy again knowing she's still hanging on, hopefully healing enough to withstand the next surge of energy that will inevitably come.

After a while, we get to the edge of the forest and find ourselves standing a few feet back from the edge of the street.

Tom says what I'm thinking. "Where the hell is that bastard?"

"What do you think? Split up?" Sandy asks him slightly breathless. Moving at that pace carrying Gio had taken its toll.

We wait to hear Tom's suggestion knowing full well that when it comes to plans, he's our guy.

Gio moans and the crackling begins.

Tom suddenly gets a determined look on his face. "Now we work our way through the city. If he is on our tail somehow, I'll shake him," he says before signaling for us to move on.

11

—

We make our way down the street. The moon, although it looks full, adds very little light to this
dimly lit area. As we pass a large slew of rundown
apartment buildings, I almost trip over a homeless guy lying
on the sidewalk. Huddled and seemingly unaware of our
presence, he doesn't even twitch as we make our way past.
Through the years I've been able to come to the city quite a
few times for concerts, plays, and different cultural events,
but this night, I'm getting the behind-the-scenes tour.

"That poor man," Ava says walking slowly by him.

I wait for her to catch up to me and watch as Guida
glances over at the man quizzically. As if feeling her gaze
drift over him, he looks up at Guida as she continues to walks
on. What was that about, I wonder to myself?

I hear it and know before it even comes around the corner. The predictable rev of the overpowered engine, as if the
only motivation it understands is full throttle.

"It's that black car," I yell as I watch it speed past us
before hearing the inevitable screeching of tires as the driver
slams on its brakes about fifty yards away.

How did it find me?

"Oh shit, this way," Tom shouts and motions for us to
head to some abandoned-looking RV parked to the side of
the street. He quickly does something with the lock on the
door and it opens. Jack of all trades, I think as I watch him
duck in the vehicle.

In a few seconds, he's leaning out the door helping Ava

climb the small narrow stairs, then Guida. The black car has turned around and is headed our way. Sandy practically throws Gio at Tom just as the car jumps the curb, speeding down the sidewalk toward us.

I freeze as it heads straight for me.

Sandy's there then, shoving me at the stairs as he yells my name. It's his voice that spurs me into action. I clumsily make my way quickly up the stairs as he pushes me from behind, closing the crappy plastic door behind him.

I immediately flinch fully expecting to feel the blunt force of the car ramming itself into the side of us. I've never encountered anything so hell-bent on my destruction before.

"Where did it go?" I hear Tom ask and look up to find him staring out the passenger side window. Sandy does a quick double take as he looks around then heads to the driver's seat. It only takes him a minute of fumbling around under the steering wheel and the engine comes to life.

"Hold on," he yells right before the camper jolts and begins to sputter down the road.

"Isn't this the weirdest camper you've ever seen?" Ava says suddenly.

I turn around to get a look and my mouth drops open. It seems as though we've all just stepped into some sort of motorized sex room.

"What the...," I mutter under my breath.

Positioned prominently in the back of the vehicle is a huge round bed with an oddly shaped metal headboard. Satiny red sheets with fuzzy purple pillows contrast the ceiling and walls, which are covered in some sort of black velvety material trimmed with shiny silver designs. Designs that remind me of...

Oh my god, I think, when I realize what I'm looking at. I quickly look away only to spot the large black and white photograph hanging above the bed. A photograph of one woman licking the nipples of another, adorned on either side by wall-length mirrors.

We turn a corner and I reach out and grab a railing attached to the ceiling that runs the whole length of the vehicle. Why is this here?

Gio moans. She's propped up next to Ava on a cushioned bench that's over by the door.

Tom and I both go to her. "Let's lay her on the bed," I say and I help Tom gently pick her up and place her on the bed's cold, slick sheets.

I feel the engine steady out as we continue down the road. Ava comes over and sits down next to her. Taking Gio's hand, she leans over and whispers in her ear, "We'll be there soon and Gregor will get you all fixed up."

Tom motions for me to follow him to the front by Sandy. Guida sits on the other side of Gio and stares at her chest. For a moment, I get the feeling she's going to do something to help Gio ... maybe something magical. Instead she just looks up at me with an odd expression.

"This has to be the most bodacious pleasure cruiser I've ever seen," Tom says as we get to the front of the camper.

"Pleasure cruiser?" I ask wondering how many vehicles like this he's seen.

"How's Gio?" Sandy asks, instantly changing the subject.

"As good as can be expected," Tom says with a sigh.

Sandy glances at the side mirror. "I don't see it, but I'm sure that car's still tailing us. We're going to have to get a little creative making our way to the warehouse without being followed."

"No sweat ... done it tons of times," Tom says. "Your best bet is to take old Smithville Road around the city and head into the warehouse district from the back. It's a dark, deserted, crap road, but less chance of our friend being able to blend in with traffic."

I wince when I hear the crackling of Gio's torture cycle start up again. It's not the awful sound of the contrived electricity that gets to me, but knowing what it's doing to her.

Sandy stiffens.

"I'm sure she's going be fine," Tom says awkwardly to him. Sandy doesn't say a word as he stares expressionless at the road ahead.

Tom turns his head away from us to stare out the passenger window. For a moment, I think that he'll stay like that the whole drive. No arguing between him and Sandy, no awkward conversations.

I realize I'm not going to be so lucky when Tom turns toward me. "You know, all the crap Harrison said about destiny or whatever, normally, I'd think the kid's off his rocker, but I gotta say, with what I've seen lately..."

There's that word again—destiny. I remember what Guida had said about Sandy and I and glance up toward the rearview mirror. I catch those amazing gray-blue eyes glance back at me before I quickly look away.

"Like Gio's whole situation," Tom continues. "I mean, like I said before, we needed her to set things in motion, to gain access to the two of you and Mark, and there she was, exactly where we needed her. I mean crazy ... huh?"

"Or your destiny theory," Sandy says sarcastically.

"Yeah, I know what you're thinking ... hell I'm thinking it ... especially now that I hear this shit coming out of my mouth. But I'm telling you this is something else. That Harrison kid, he knows things. Shit that nobody could know."

"If he is some sort of psychic or—"

"No, it's more than that. I mean, I've never seen anything

124

like it. Around the time Jo went in the cave Harrison starts having premonitions and shit. Not just that, he knew stuff he couldn't possibly have known, hell, answered some questions Gregor and I were still scratching our heads with, and with Gregor, that's saying a lot. I mean that guy's a genius when it comes to all this spacey science shit. I don't know, he just looks at things in amazing ways. Anyway, Harrison shows up spouting things that sound like they're right out of a science fiction novel. Those wacky-ass ones, too.

I hear the engine rev then, only it's not ours. Coming out of nowhere, the black car speeds up, coming around to the left of the RV, then slows to cruise along the side of us.

"Jo, get down," Sandy says driving the big awkward camper while trying to peer into the car's black tinted window to get a look.

The car suddenly swerves as if it's going to ram us. Sandy quickly reacts sending the cumbersome camper over to the side of the road. Ava screams and I grab for the metal bar above my head as we hit gravel, causing the vehicle to momentarily lose traction. Sandy immediately adjusts and cuts to the left. With the RV back fully on the road, it's only a second before Sandy swerves and we're headed toward the side of the black car again. It easily veers to the left avoiding our inept attempt to strike back.

"Damn," Sandy says and I can tell he's not enjoying the unwieldy maneuverability of the leisure cruiser. Probably handles a little different than his usual ride, the silver Porsche.

The car drives like that for a minute before suddenly slamming on the brakes enough that we fly by. I can't help but feel like it's taunting us ... probably wanting me to know that at some point I'll have to leave the safety of this big camper ... and when I do...

Tom points to a road ahead. "You'd normally take this

turn coming up, which would take you right into the district, but pass it and keep going. I know something we can do that'll slow this dick up a little. Might buy us some time … well, at least enough to dump this ride."

"I'd love to know who this guy is?" Sandy asks as he drives right by the road Tom pointed out.

"You're not the only one. Whoever it is, he likes to mess with our heads."

"Yeah, he's been doing that all along," I say thinking back to all the times he could have taken me out so easily but didn't. "I'm sure he wants me dead, but I'm beginning to think he wants to torture me a little first."

Gio's device begins to crackle and I instantly regret my choice of words.

"So Harrison didn't see anything about the car in his plan?" Sandy asks sarcastically.

"Awe … shit. I know what you're getting at—"

"No Tom, I don't think you do. Since when do you leave so much to chance?"

"To chance?"

"Yeah. This plan had numerous holes, like … like how could you have known I would go to Gio when she texted?"

"Are you kidding? You forget Sandy … I know you."

"What does that mean?"

"That means I had zero fucking doubt you'd go if you thought Gio was in trouble. Even with your unpredictable behavior lately, I knew you wouldn't let her down. Not you … not ever."

"I don't buy it. I know you have that knack for reading people but even so, you normally wouldn't have put so much faith in it. Not when dealing with The Order."

"Yeah well … a lot's changed lately, hell … in the last twenty-four hours. I mean, The Order's old news … well, should be about now anyway."

I'm shocked to hear it and ask, "But how?"

"Joshua, the kid you met running all my surveillance, released a virus into The Order's main frame. I don't know the specifics, but everything should be fried nice and crispy by now."

"All this time and that's all it took to take them down?" I ask incredulously.

"I wish. When Jo was going through her change they realized something was happening to the power source. The assholes started scrambling, making mistakes. Mistakes that Gregor and I helped along, of course."

"Of course," Sandy says, not surprised.

"That's about the time Irina started to go loopy, the death of her son and all," he says avoiding my gaze.

"Mitchell used that opportunity to advance his own agenda, which threw the whole system out of whack. Like a fucking house of cards," he says and chuckles.

"What did you do with Irina," I ask already knowing the answer, at least hoping so anyway.

He glances back at Ava. She's totally engrossed in Gio's ordeal.

Whispering he says, "Ava being able to transport some- one to a place she's been was honestly my best option. I didn't have the time to figure out where to put Irina, to babysit the bitch, so she didn't cause me any more trouble, so I went with plan B. While you two were chasing Mark up to the lab, I had someone that had been working for me on the inside bring her to me. Then I had Ava transport her to a vehicle Ava had ridden in with me days ago. Nothing special about it then, so Ava didn't give it a second thought ... and I never want her to. I never want her knowing that I took that ve- hicle, made it so the doors and windows would never open again and sunk it. Sunk it somewhere nobody would think to look. So to answer your question, ... I took her out.

I wonder then how many people would have loved that honor.

"Your turn's coming up," Tom says suddenly.

Sandy slows the vehicle, but with all the road construction signs it's hard to tell which road is a viable one.

"Turn there," he says pointing to a road behind a huge orange and black Road Closed sign.

Sandy turns without question. As we speed on, the camper hitting one pothole after another, Gio moans periodically. How long can her body keep taking the punishment?

"I'm going in the garage," Sandy asks as we come up to the edge of the district.

"Yeah, the fucker will easily follow us through the first barrier but then shouldn't be able to make it past the last two. Let's just hope Joshua didn't put our systems on lockdown."

"Why would he do that?" I ask.

"Safety precaution. If he or Gregor happened to notice I suddenly disappeared. Remember, I wasn't supposed to be on your end of things.

Sandy suddenly slows way down as we come into the warehouse district. Although the rest of the city is lit up, this area is dark and gloomy with most of the old lampposts burned out or busted. Faded for sale signs adorn the sides of most of the buildings.

"You haven't been out here in a while," Tom says to Sandy.

"No, but still as charming as I remember."

Tom snickers. "Yeah, but I'll miss the seedy underworld feel of this place and the perspective it always gave me."

"Miss it?"

"Told you, things have changed. Just recently sold the

Ellipse Group to the highest bidder and made a shitload of money."

"What about the other places around here?"

"Just ditching the rest, that is except Gregor's lab. You've never seen that place. It was a shitty warehouse, kind of like everything else around here, until Gregor got his hands on it. You'll be shocked at what he's got up there now."

Sandy stops the vehicle. "We're getting near the entrance. Jo, can you hear anything?"

I listen, half-expecting to hear the predictable hum of the black car's supercharged engine, but instead just hear the crackling of Gio's torture device kicking on.

"I don't hear the car."

"You sure about this?" Sandy asks Tom.

"Sure about the fact that we don't have a hell of a lot of options," Tom says.

Sandy turns the RV down a short side street coming to a stop in front of a security gate. As our weight triggers the mechanism, I watch as the arm slowly rises allowing us to enter an outside parking area. Parked over to the side are a number of trucks with the words The Ellipse Group written on the side. Sandy drives through the lot slowly, looking in the mirrors for any sign that we are being followed.

"I don't see the asshole but I know he's out there," Tom says eyeing Sandy.

We pull up and stop right in front of a large bronzed metal garage door, shining and new in contrast to the aging, dilapidated construction of the attached structure.

"I'll punch in the code and hope that I can get the door down behind you before any unwelcome guests," Tom says opening the passenger door.

"Watch yourself, he doesn't always stay in the car," Sandy says.

"Wonderful," Tom says and hops out, closing the door behind him.

He goes right up to a number pad and swiftly enters and code. The door begins to lift ever so slowly as we wait anxiously. Why are these garage doors so damn slow, I think, wondering if I'd be able to get to Tom in time if the need be.

The door's up and we pull in quicker than this monstrous vehicle should. As soon as we clear the entrance, the door begins to close behind us with its same sluggish pace. Once closed completely, Tom jumps back into the vehicle.

"We're all clear."

I head to the back of the camper with Sandy and Tom following. Guida is expressionless as Ava sits beside Gio holding her hand in an attempt to comfort her while she heals from the last torture session.

"That thing in her … it's so awful," Ava says, her eyes filling with tears.

Sandy puts his hand on her shoulder. "We'll get her to Gregor."

Tom eyes Ava and in an uncharacteristically tender manner says, "Don't worry sunshine, we're not that far now."

Her whole mood seems to brighten with his words, and I watch Guida's eyes do their freakish movement suddenly, as she digests the exchange.

"We're going to get into the warehouse—one way or another," Tom says then looks my way. "Jo, you bring up the rear. If we are being followed, he'll come up from behind."

Sandy gently picks up Gio, securing her in his arms.

"Let's go," Tom says without another word, and we follow him out of the camper and into the garage. I instantly feel vulnerable without the cocoon-like feel of the pleasure cruiser. I must not be the only one, I think, as I watch Ava grab Tom's hand.

Tom, pulling Ava by the hand, heads over to a door on the side of the garage. There's a number pad mounted on the wall next to it. He punches in a code and the light on the pad goes from red to green.

He opens the door and walks through with each of us following. We find ourselves in another surveillance room with ten different monitors set up displaying the security feeds of locations all around this area.

"This alley is the best way to go," Tom says to Sandy pointing at a monitor. "I figure one of our friend's M.O.'s is stealth, so we'll go a way that takes that out of the equation for him. None of those nooks and crannies to hide in. Just a straight shot from here to an underground club attached to the warehouse. Once inside the club, I can get us in the warehouse through a secured door located in the owner's main office."

"Will the owner let us in?" I ask wondering what kind of underground club it is. I've heard of all kinds of themed clubs located around here. Way out there, crazy kind of clubs.

"Won't be a problem this time of night. By this hour, she'll never notice."

The device attached to Gio stops its cycle, but she doesn't moan this time. Just lets out a barely audible ragged breath.

"I don't know how much more she can take," Sandy says, wrapping up our planning session.

Tom sighs, then heads over to another door with an alarm mechanism attached and punches in the code. As I hear the tunes of the numbers, I realize this is a different code altogether. Does every door have a different code? How does he keep them all straight? I wonder as I follow everyone out of the door, bringing up the rear on this expedition to safety.

We walk out to the street and head to the alley with Tom and Ava leading, Guida right behind them, as Sandy carries

Gio. Listening intently, I try to pick up on any noise other than the distinct trot of our shoes against the old time brick road made up of small brown bricks with pitted grooves throughout.

Even as we move forward, I find myself glancing around as the dark, shadowy buildings cast eerie shapes all around us. I can just make out the lettering on an old-fashioned faded sign above a boarded-up door. I see the word Meat and cringe. They did something with meat in there?

I can see where some of the bricks on these run-down abandoned buildings have been painted over years ago. So long ago that I can see patches of bricks throughout as the paint has had time to peel away. Time has turned the metal borders framing each dingy window rusty.

No one says a word as we move along, getting closer to what I'm starting to hear as a faint booming sound, the odd rhythm of music from what I can only hope is our intended destination. Looking down the street, I notice that one of the buildings has crumbled in on one side, leaving me wondering how safe these structures really are.

Tom slows and points just up ahead to a small black door made of iron. That must be the entrance.

We get to the iron door and Tom says over the strange music, "Prepare yourselves," then knocks loudly.

What does he mean by that?

Standing there waiting for someone to come to a door that I never in a million years would have imagined myself at, I take it all in. This entire area seems like it should be condemned, yet here is some underground club, obviously thriving. It's safe to assume that the police or city officials must not care what happens to the patrons of this bizarre establishment. Either that or someone's getting paid to look the other way. Again, too many cop shows...

I hear a lock snap and the door opens. Tom steps forward and says something in the ear of the largest and strangest-looking woman I've ever seen. Spiked white hair with black roots adorn the face of a woman in her late twenties. She's dressed in a black leather pantsuit with red stitching following its way around her breasts and waist. Her face has piercings in places I never thought possible. All of this pales in comparison to her eyes—a glowing bright red.

The woman motions for us to enter the club. She holds the door as we all pile in. Once past a narrow passageway, we come to a pair of large, oddly ornate iron doors similar to the front door. The music is not only louder now but much stranger as I follow the others through the doors entering a tremendously large area that must be the club itself.

I quickly scan the room as my senses jump to high alert. It only takes a few seconds then my mouth drops open as I realize what I'm looking at.

Vampires.

12

---

ong greasy dark hair pulled back into a low ponytail belongs to the man hovering threateningly over a woman. Wearing lingerie made of sheer white material she's lying on her back across a white velvet settee. She throws her shoulder-length blond tresses backward suddenly as he lowers his head to the unnaturally pale skin of her upper thigh. All eyes in the room are fixated on this couple on top of the stage to my right.

Grabbing Ava's hand, Tom pulls her away. I glance at Guida wondering what she thinks of this spectacle and find her looking around the room perplexed by it all.

The room has grown silent even as the heavy Goth music blares on. Following the others through the club, I can't help but glance back at the stage. Trails of blood are running down the woman's leg from two puncture wounds now present on the inside of her right thigh. As the observers react in unison to the conclusion of the skit, she lays there motionless, the victim in this deviant display.

"Bunch of freaks wishing they were vampires," Tom says under his breath then stops short. Turning, I hear him say to Ava, "Just keep your eyes down, sunshine."

Ava nods and averts her eyes away from a man staring at her a few feet away. Bald with a strange tattoo on the side of his neck, his eyes completely blacked out, he doesn't blink as he fixates on her. Good call Tom, I think as I step between her and his line of sight.

I sneak a glance at Sandy, but he's all business. Holding

Gio, he's scanning the room, looking right past all this out-landishness. A few people eye him curiously. I guess him standing there holding a passed-out girl would normally be considered strange, but it doesn't garner him so much as a second look from a lot of people here.

The club is pure Goth. Black reinforced steel beams sporadically placed throughout the club run from the black painted concrete floors to the four-story ceilings. The windows have been blacked out.

In contrast to the stark black backdrop is the old-world brothel decor. Light-diffusing red glass sconces hang on the walls throughout, casting a warm light on the vampire-in-spired artwork. My eyes then fall on bouquets of dead flowers positioned throughout the room.

In the center of the club is a large area that's packed with bodies moving to the odd, rhythmic patterns of the music, connected to one another in an almost ritualistic trancelike state. I continue to follow the others around to the left past an area where red velvet settees surround a large metal bar. Hanging above the bar is a large glass cabinet held in place by two giant black cables connected all the way to the ex-tremely tall ceiling. Housed inside the cabinet are dozens of exquisitely ornate wineglasses flooded by a sea of red light coming from a recess in the top of the case. I've never seen such an amazing display just for glasses.

Two male bartenders standing behind the bar tower above the patrons as they serve drinks wearing nothing but black pants made from the same material as the hostess's out-fit. Built like Olympians, they too have bright red eyes. A dress code, I take it.

Getting a closer look at their customers, I do a double take. Most are sporting a pair of sharp-looking fangs, Gothic clothes and a pair of what I can only assume are colored contacts. I catch the gaze of a guy with ethereal light-blue contacts and he catches my own eyes, seemingly impressed. I realize of all the places in the world Guida and I could have walked into, this is the one place where our eyes would bring with it a level of normalcy.

Observing one of the bartenders serving drinks, I notice most people are sipping from the same fancy wineglasses held on display in the cabinet. Each one is filled with a red liquid. If I were watching a vampire movie, I'd instantly think blood, but this is real life. People don't drink blood in real life. Regardless of the red liquid, seeing the wineglass up close makes me want to hold one in my hand. To trace my finger along the pewter design that envelops the pitted glass of the goblet.

Leaving the bar area, we make our way toward a hallway in the back of the club. I can't help but feel like Count Dracula himself could have had a hand in the interior decorating. We get to the hall, but before going down it, Tom stops walking and turns around.

"These people take this pretend shit to a whole new level, huh?" Tom says snickering. "You know, I should get my hands on one of those real looking movie production werewolves, just to freak 'em out." I chuckle at the thought.

On the dance floor, bright red lights dance with the rhythm of the music, making the entire scene seem more chaotic. It's some kind of laser strobe light that must have kicked on when the music changed. Feeling slightly uneasy, my pulse quickens and I catch a quick glimpse of a dark figure flash through the crowd. Just as quickly, their gone. What the heck...

Then I hear the familiar sound and pull my head back. Two discs lodge themselves into the wall right next to my head. Ava gasps as I recognize them immediately.

"He's here," I yell to the others.

"Get to the room in the back," Tom says motioning for us to run by him and make our way down the dimly lit hallway to a black door at the very end. Ava and Guida do as instructed, but I stop. Indecision holds me in its grip.

"Go on," Tom says to me.

"Get Gio to Gregor. I'll hold him off," I say wondering how exactly I'm going to hold off someone I can never seem to see.

Sandy practically throws Gio at Tom. "Take her to Gregor."

Sandy doesn't need to say anything else for Tom to understand his intentions: protect Jo at all costs.

We make sure Tom is through the door, then I quickly step out into the room before Sandy has a chance to say otherwise.

Looking up at the wall, my heart sinks when I see the metal discs are gone. Left behind are two deep cuts in the wall where the long serrated edges were.

This person's like a freaking phantom, I think as I head to a dark corner in the back of the club. I need to get into a better position, but with all these people around it's going to be hard to see who our attacker is.

The stage up front is empty as the night's festivities have made a drastically loud turn. The hardcore pulse of the music has the dance floor crowded as everyone moves to the indistinct words of the singer. His voice is one minute a smooth monotonic baritone, before breaking into a screaming rant. Feeling unnerved by it, I don't hear the metal discs fly by me and find their intended target.

Sandy grunts as the weapons pierce his chest. He reaches up and yanks the first disc out. The gash that's left behind begins to bleed instantly.

"Sandy–"

"I'm fine," he says irritated.

I grab it from his hand and push a small button in the center. The serrated blades instantly retract, leaving a smaller and smoother disc. So that's how this idiot can carry these things around with him, I think and toss it to the ground feeling peeved.

"Watch out," Sandy yells, pulling me to him just as two more of the lethal discs fly by me. He rips the second from his body as he pushes me down with him. Kneeling on the ground now, I survey the room quickly. How are we supposed to fight someone we can't even see?

"I'd like to know how many of these things he has," Sandy says studying the disc for a moment before tossing it away.

I notice the blood right under the two slashes on the front of his shirt. After seeing what they did to the wall, I can only imagine how it felt to have them slice into his chest.

The thought of Sandy getting hurt feeds my anger. If this asshole wants me, then he'll get me, I think as I jump up moving toward the bar area.

I see him then, that same dark figure as before standing on the edge of the dance floor. Slight in stature, he's dressed in all black with a hood that casts a shadow over his face.

I take off in his direction realizing Sandy's right behind. It's only a second and we're there, but he's gone, vanished again. God he's fast. I'm not even able to look behind me before I hear Sandy's breath catch and feel the pain in my arm—a disc embedded just above my elbow. Spinning around, I see Sandy's been struck by another disc too.

"He's got to be one of our kind," I say.

Sandy yanks the disc out of my arm in one fluid motion and tosses it to the ground. He's pissed. Two guys bump into me then as they jump around crazily to the Goth rock. I catch sight of him standing motionless near the bar, as if waiting for something.

I move in his direction, knowing he won't stay still long and also knowing that any minute he's going to bombard me with those razor-sharp discs. In one swift motion, he jumps up on the bar and begins to run down the length of it away from me. The bartenders gawk as he gets to the end of the bar and without slowing up, flips into the air, and onto the ground. Without even a second's delay, he's off headed away from me again.

Its not the speed or agility with which this person moves that has me amazed but the fact that somewhere in the two seconds it took to flip off the bar he was able to send two discs flying my way.

I thwart their desired effect easily, but Sandy, right on my tail again, doesn't. I pause to glance back at Sandy, and our assailant quickly melds back into the crowd of dancers.

Irritated, Sandy rips the blades out yet again.

The fact that this guy hasn't hit anyone else here, even by accident, is incredible. Actually, it's almost impossible.

With the lights pulsating all around us we enter the dance floor. As I scan the area I get a glimpse of him on the other side of it, again just standing ... taunting us.

"We need to change our tactic if we're going to get this guy," Sandy says.

The crowd shifts and the man vanishes.

Sandy's hit again. He curses and shakes his head at me like he just can't believe it. He's right, this is getting old.

Sandy yanks the discs out as I catch sight of our hooded friend again, standing motionless as the bodies around him move up and down.

That's when I notice Sandy's breathing starts to become labored.

"Jo, I think there was something on the blades," Sandy says, his eyelids drooping. Something on the blades ... like a toxin? This person may be deadlier than I thought.

Sandy stumbles to the edge of the dance floor. As I reach for him, he falls to the ground, a heap at my feet.

"Sandy," I yell, trying to keep him awake as I cradle his head in my hands. I notice a few people beginning to take notice to our display but ignore them as I feel my emotions beginning to take hold.

His eyes close, but he's still breathing ... still alive. My eyes rove over him as he lays here motionless. Hit so many times by those damn discs that his shirt looks like it was used in the production of a horror movie. All the while sticking by my side, thinking only to protect me.

I feel the rage well up inside me at the injustice of it all. Standing, I turn toward the crowd. Other than a small group watching us as if believing it to be another odd skit, most are still unaware of anything else going on around them other than their own rhythmic movements. I search for my adversary. I see a flash of movement come from somewhere on the other side of this horde of bodies.

Somewhere deep within me I know that the only thing standing in the way of getting my hands on this stealthy enemy are the club-goers. The floor needs to be cleared.

I feel myself act on my ambitions. The energy source within me, the one that feeds all my abilities, reacts. Instinctively, I thrust my hands out in front of me and in one complete motion push them toward the floor. There's a flash of amber light and at that very instant everyone in the entire club hits the floor. Glancing up, I realize the scope of my power. The only man left standing is the one I'm hunting.

The red lights bounce all around us as the music plays on. The man reaches up and I brace myself for a strike. Instead he pulls his hood back. I take a couple steps forward, amazed by what I think I see. Shoulder-length jet-black hair with red tips frame the face of a girl who couldn't be more than eighteen.

Even though I see her standing there, it takes me a minute to wrap my head around the fact that it's been a girl this whole time.

As if used to my reaction, she smiles, her extremely full lips revealing an almost perfect set of white teeth. Perfect except for the unusually noticeable eyeteeth. Cool, but odd, I think before snapping back to reality.

A second later, her smile fades—she's noticed my eyes.

We face off, just like in those old-timey Western movies, sizing each other up, getting ready to strike at any moment.

She moves and I follow. Cocking my head to the right, the discs fly by as I close the gap between us. She reaches one of the black reinforced beams and, grabbing it, swings around it. Her feet connect with me, completely knocking me back onto one of the velvet settees. There's a flash of light followed by a sharp pain to the side of my head as I feel her kick me, causing my entire body to shift to the right. I barely get my eyes open before I see her foot headed my way again, this time connecting with the side of my mouth. My head jerks to the side.

I scramble to avoid the next blow and feel the air shift as she misses her mark. It throws her off just long enough, and I do the only thing I can think of—I tackle her. We both go flying toward the bar with her taking the brunt of it in her back. It seems to knock the wind out of her just long enough for me to raise my fist to punch her in the face. Even with her lack of oxygen, she's fast. In one fluid motion, she blocks my punch and gets to her feet.

Expecting her to attack again, I face her, ready this time. Noticing my determination she gives me a slight nod and pulls two short spearlike weapons out of her jacket. What's with the nod, and what else does she have in there, I wonder?

I watch her twirl them around in a menacing fashion, as if warming up for something. I have a good idea what she's going to try to do with those. I can tell she's a professional. Although seemingly young, she's been trained and trained well.

She stops her display and, holding the spears on either side of her face, she nods. I leap onto the bar, like I have some sort of natural catlike tendency to head to high ground when faced with danger.

She easily follows, and now we're both on top of the bar, facing each other. Waving those little spears around threateningly, she slowly comes toward me as I stumble backward, trying to think of a way to keep their sharp edges from finding their way into me.

Just then, my foot hits the edge of the bar. I'm out of time, I have to do something.

There's a loud pop and then cracking begins above the girl. As she looks up, shards of glass start raining down on her. She jumps out of the way of the heavy downpour but not before being pummeled with the smashed fragments of the glass cabinet mixed with the metal pieces of broken wineglasses.

There's Sandy, standing by a pile of dead flowers. The same flowers that must have fallen out of the vase he just chucked at the cabinet.

The girl, blood running down the side of her head, regains her senses quickly. She swipes down and grabs one of the short spears she dropped.

With a spear in each hand, she runs up to Sandy and quickly stabs at his head.

Sandy surprises me by deflecting each of her strikes easily. Before I'm even consciously aware, I'm right beside her.

I grab her by the hair, yanking her backward to the ground.

That's when I feel something stir within me.

The second before I shove my hand into her chest, I see her stare into my eyes in a state of shock. Then the vision comes.

Reaching out, the cool stone wall warms under my touch as I make my way through the narrow ingress.

I see her then, kneeling ... praying. She doesn't move as the dark shadow comes up behind her, but not a shadow...

I yell to her, but she doesn't move. I yell again when I see light refract off the tip of the blade, raised high above her head.

Her eyes open suddenly. Wide open as if surprised, she just stares at me.

I pull my hand back when I realize my vision has become reality. The girl, now gasping for breath, is still staring up at me in the same surprised state.

An eerie silence fills the room. The song that a moment ago was vibrating the walls must have ended while she and I were connected in our vision quest. With the DJ presumably unconscious on the floor, the lights continue to dance around to the silence.

Sandy comes over to me. "Are you all right?"

"Yeah, are you?"

He nods. "I feel fine now," he says bending down to check the pulse of a woman lying on the floor.

"Alive, just passed out I guess," he says and smiles reassuringly at me.

Relief courses through me when I realize I didn't kill all these people. But what did I do to them?

He looks at the girl, "So you..."

"Yeah. Her," I say looking at Sandy in disbelief.

"I'd say she's just as shocked as you."

My mind tries to wrap around the fact that I branded her—her, of all people?

Wide-eyed and still struggling to regain her composure, she stands up. I can tell she's working through it all. What's odd is that she doesn't look at the brand, doesn't seem at all interested in it. She just stares at me, as if surprised. Probably trying to figure out what the hell I just did to her.

As if to prove me wrong, she suddenly says in the most stoic manner possible, "I am honored to have been chosen."

"Chosen?"

"As one of the twelve," she says humbly, her green eyes looking at me as if still deciphering it all.

I look at Sandy, shocked. How does she know about the twelve?

She continues, "Although you are not the person I was expecting to–"

"We better get out of here," Sandy says suddenly, and I immediately notice why. The people in the room are starting to stir.

For a moment, Sandy seems perplexed about what to do with the girl. Five minutes ago, she was trying to kill us, and now she's part of this whole thing.

"Let's go," he says making up his mind.

We quickly follow him through the club and down the narrow hallway. Entering the same black door the others went through earlier, we find ourselves in a surprisingly spacious office with the same high ceilings we've seen throughout the warehouse. Decorated with the same motif as the rest of the club, there's the largest desk I've ever seen sitting right in the middle of the room. The manager's desk, I can only assume. It's dark wood with iron ornamentation, the kind you would see in one of those ancient cemeteries. Whoever sits behind that thing is either really important or at least thinks they are.

I hear music start blaring again from inside the club.

"Sounds like things are going again out there," Sandy says.

I glance at the door half-expecting someone to bust through any moment. Someone has to wonder what the heck happened. I mean, I know weird things happen in this club, but come on.

There's a loud clicking noise and a section of the back wall opens. "A secret doorway, but how did Tom know–"

"He has hidden security cameras all over this area," Sandy says matter-of-factly as if used to Tom and his watch-dog ways.

Heading for the door that's now open, I'm hardly through it when I see him coming right at me. My breath catches as he rushes to me, pulling me to him tightly. The moment I wrap my arms around him, that horrible feeling, the edge I feel when we're separated, begins to melt away as he holds me close. At this moment, I could care less about all the crazy things that have happened tonight. All I care about is that I'm back with him—back with Mark.

13

—

"THANK GOD," HE WHISPERS IN MY ear. We hold on to each other, comforted by the fact that we're both safe and together again. I feel like our entire relationship revolves around being together and safe.

Pulling away, I break our small reprieve to examine him. "Are you still—"

"I'm fine ... see," he says then pulls up his shirt showing me his white bandage.

"Give me one second," we hear someone say suddenly.

Joshua, the tech guy, is sitting behind a computer monitor, his fingers flying over the keys at such a speed that I'm reminded that although he's not one of the chosen, he's still one of us. I watch as page after page of cryptic-looking number-laden information flash on the screen. His hands are a blur.

"Ok, done," he says and hits the last key with more gusto than anyone should. Immediately, I hear a faint click of the door we just came through and can only assume he's put everything back the way it was before.

"Who's she?" Mark asks me quietly as he notices the new girl standing next to Sandy.

"Uh, that's kind of a long story."

"One I have recorded," Joshua says and smiles. "Tom's going to really enjoy watching that video file."

"Jo, you're going to need to prepare yourself," Mark says then, and by the look on his face my hearts drops.

"Where is she," Sandy asks immediately, seeming to know what he's talking about even before Mark says it.

That's when I remember ... Gio.

"This way," Joshua says as he heads out of the room. Mark doesn't let go of my hand as we leave the room and walk down a narrow hallway.

"I don't know if you know this, Jo, but Gregor was the scientist that formed The Circle," Joshua says as if suddenly becoming a tour guide. He put together this warehouse lab and brought Tom on board. I honestly don't think you could find two people more different, but the stuff they've accomplished ... whoa, it's insanely impressive."

I think about Joshua and his part in all this. He's obviously enamored with Tom and Gregor, but from what I've seen him do, it seems he has just as much a hand in all their progress. We leave the hallway and enter a large main room. This warehouse space is part of the same building as the club.

Right away I spot Harrison, his arm around Ava, seemingly comforting her. Guida, with her distracting beauty, just stands beside them, her strange eyes appearing to lock on our new team member as we head toward them.

Ava spots us then and runs to Sandy, throwing her arms around his neck.

"It's been awful, just awful," she says as she starts to cry. Sandy holds her, not saying a word as he stares off to the side of the room. I notice what he's looking at and my breath catches in my throat.

On the other end of the room, I see Gregor and Tom standing over a body lying on a table. Even from this distance, I can hear the beeping of a machine and make out the periodic curse words coming from Tom.

Sandy gives Ava one last reassuring squeeze and smile before breaking free of her grasp and heading over.

"Go ahead Jo, I'll take care of her," I hear Harrison say in my head right before he reaches for her hand.

Mark and I follow Sandy across the room while the new girl, sensitive to the situation, stays with the others, observing from a distance. My nerves become edgy when I hear Ava start to sob again.

Tom, not missing a thing, raises his eyebrows at me when he notices the new girl. Holding some sort of suctioning instrument, he's standing over Gio as she lies on an examination table, her luscious dark hair falling in cascades off the table around her.

I see her body twitch every so often as Gregor, his back to us, works feverishly on something in her midsection.

Sandy goes around the other side of her and scans the scene. It's the look on his face that stops me in my tracks. I've seen and done so many things over the last few days, but am I really prepared to see Gio like this? As irritating as she's been to me, I would feel horrible if anything were to happen to her. And Sandy, I know, would be devastated.

Mark and I just stand there watching it all from a few feet away. The area around her has been set up like a makeshift operating room. Bloodied towels are on the floor beside a small table that's holding a few sharp-looking medical instruments.

As Gregor bends over her body, Tom lowers the suction instrument to the area Gregor's honed in on. I squeeze Mark's hand.

Sandy watches the scene intensely, the guilt he feels so evident in his gaze. He's so loyal to those he cares about. It would kill me to see him hurting. I would do anything to save him from that ... anything. I feel the urge to go over and reassure him, hug him, anything that would make it all better for him.

"I've just about got it," Gregor says but then suddenly pulls his hands away from her as the sound of the device's electrical current begins. Although much more of a gargle this time, I can still faintly make out the device's distinctive crackling noise.

"I don't like the sound of that," Tom says eying Gregor oddly.

"The device's structural integrity is beginning to break down. If I don't get it out of her by the next cycle—"

The noise stops and Gregor immediately dives back into the process of removing it from her chest. He seems more on edge as he labors over what I can only assume are the intricate details of his work. Tom's silence is proof of his anxiety. All I can do is hold my breath, knowing that Gio's fate rests with him.

I wonder what Mark thinks as he watches his dad, a man who was wanted, needed by so many but couldn't possibly be there for them all. Was it ever realistic to expect a man with his talents to push it all aside for the interpersonal workings of a family? Is he even capable of it?

Breaking my oddly timed contemplative moment, Gregor suddenly raises something out of her. About the size of a child's fist, it's dripping blood as he carries it over and places it on the table.

"Now for the cloth," he says bending down and grabbing a small towel out of a bucket of liquid. "We have to put this cloth over the opening in her chest until she's healed," he says wringing out the excess liquid before draping it over her.

"Will it work?" Tom asks.

"It should," Gregor says.

"What happened?" Sandy asks.

"What should have been a simple retrieval of the implant wasn't. When I first attempted to take it out, something in the device malfunctioned, which triggered an exponential increase in the electrical output."

"She was basically frying," Tom interjects.

Gregor nods. "Yes, she was. Her organs were about to combust. I had no choice but to try to counter the trigger and reinsert it until I could figure out a way around it."

"So she'll heal?" Sandy asks.

"That's the hope. The power source within us is electrical by nature so I formulated a liquid that should help as a mild conductor for the healing process. That cloth I draped over her had been saturated in it. Just how much help her body needs to heal though at this point is hard to say. After what she's been through, honestly, I can't be sure she'll even fully recover."

Sandy looks sick as Gregor's words sink in. Squeezing Mark's hand, I let go then head over to the side of the table. I feel a lump in my throat as I notice blood has already soaked through the wet towel covering her. The monitors continue to beep in a slow rhythm. I can only assume it's monitoring her heart rate or breathing or something. Whatever it's keeping track of, I'm sure the constant beeping is a good thing.

For a moment, no one says anything as we all stand around, each of us lost in our own thoughts, as we listen to what we can only hope is affirmation that Gio's body is healing.

A second later and Tom inquiring about the new girl to Sandy.

"Jo, how is she?" I hear Harrison ask in my head.

Shouldn't he know, I mean if he's psychic or whatever?

"My abilities are still fuzzy at times, and again, always connected to you. Maybe because Gio's condition doesn't affect you I'm not seeing anything. I don't know," he says sounding frustrated.

I instantly feel bad for my thoughts. I have to remember he's a kid that's been given abilities that aren't cut and dry.

That and the fact that he can hear everything I think, that alone would be enough to send someone over the edge.

"It's not that bad. It's better than being in Tom's head all the time," he says and I see him smile from across the room where he and the others are standing.

Noticing Ava and how anxious she seems I quickly answer Harrison's initial question.

"Gregor was able to get the device out. Now it's up to her body to heal," I say in my head then hear Harrison say the same thing to the others.

It takes me a minute to realize what I just did. I don't know what's weirder; the fact that I have super hearing and can talk to Harrison just with my thoughts, or the fact that I've already come to rely on these abilities.

Guida's beside me then, looking down at Gio in the strangest way. Suddenly I notice her eyes' odd movements become more sporadic. The monitors react.

"What the hell's happening?" Tom asks as we all quickly take a step back to allow Gregor to access her and the machines. Sandy stares intensely at him, his scrutiny laden with expectation. Gregor, oblivious to anything but the task at hand, quickly begins to push buttons on the monitor to figure out what is happening.

Gio lies unresponsive to the activity happening around her. Her beautiful dark hair framing her face is the exact hue of her eyelashes. Long and thick, they fan across her face in stark contrast to her skin, which is now a ghostly white instead of its usual olive perfection.

"We're losing her," Gregor says bluntly, his tone implying that he must not have a whole lot of options for saving her life. I gasp as he rips off the cloth from her chest exposing a hole within her chest cavity. Rushing over to the bucket of liquid, he dunks the cloth in.

Guida glances my way. The look on her face makes me feel as though I should be doing something. But what can I do?

"Jo, I don't think Gio's going to heal without your help," Harrison says sounding odd.

"My help? How am I supposed to help her ..."

I glance over at him and see him holding his head in his hand as if in pain. He's a having a vision and like he says, they're always about me. Now I know I'm getting ready to do something.

"I think she's going," Tom exclaims when Gregor comes back over with the cloth and places it back over Gio's wound.

The monitors' alarm suddenly stops, replaced by a steady drone. The sound when it's no longer detecting a heartbeat or life of any kind.

"Oh shit ... Jo's eyes," I hear Tom exclaim. All eyes turn toward me, and before anyone can protest I send everyone back away from the table in one fluid motion as I instinctively reach for Gio. I hear the monitors come alive right before everything disappears.

Halting abruptly, I turn and wait for her to catch up. Her challenges are getting better but I still beat her easily, even though I don't always want to.

Senses heightening, I glance around knowing the lush green surroundings can't trick me with their comfort. I quickly become edgy when I notice the subtle movements of the landscape. She wants me out here ... it's another aspect of her test.

I feel her presence moments before I see her.

Out of breath, she laughs, egging me on again with just her demeanor.

"You can't beat me at everything," she says then. "I love him too..."

She takes off running, and although her words hit me in

the gut, it's these mental pushes that keep me sharp ... ready.

Gregor's voice fades into my conscienceless before anything else.

"Whatever she's doing is working," I hear him say breathlessly then blink as the scene floods back in. Gregor's leaning against the edge of the table staring past me and up at the monitor, its steady rhythm sounding out the beat of a strong, healthy heartbeat.

"Jo," I hear Mark say right before I feel his hand on my arm. I realize then that I'm still grabbing onto Gio. I'm gripping her wrist in one hand as my other is pressed against her chest. Tinkering on the edge of the hole within her.

I instantly pull away, afraid that my touch could harm her. By the sound of the monitor and the way Gregor and the others are looking at me, I believe I've done just the opposite.

All of a sudden I'm not feeling so good.

"Her vitals are strong again," Gregor says then pulls back the cloth that's draped over her wound. It only takes him a second before he realizes the full scope of what I've done.

"The rate at which she's healed is unprecedented," Gregor says staring at me in awe. The science geek in him is pumped.

Tom, understanding immediately what I've done, finds his validation, Gio's own special brand, put there as my declaration that not only is she going to live but she's going to live for a reason.

I feel a wave of nausea course through my body. I fight the urge to vomit as I taste something familiarly sweet inside my mouth. The same taste from my change earlier in the cave.

The revolting taste is too much, and I feel my body convulse. I speed to a dark corner as my body quickly loses its sense of control. There's no stopping it. My body expels anything and everything in its quest to rid itself of whatever could be causing the awful taste to return.

Trembling as my heaves quickly become dry and empty, I sit down and lean up against the wall, closing my eyes trying to wrap my mind around the fact that I just barfed all over everything.

Opening my eyes, I'm pleasantly surprised. It's just me, alone with my small splatter of vomit. Very small splatter. I really need to eat something.

"Jo, are you all right?" I hear Mark ask at the other end of the dark hall.

I stand up and regain my composure, then make my way back to him.

Upon seeing me, he smiles. "Harrison wouldn't let me follow you. Said you wanted to be alone."

I smile back, thankful for once for Harrison's crazy mind melding ability. I realize I don't need to thank him because he knows what I'm thinking right now. My life's so weird, I think as I give Mark a slight smile, feeling completely embarrassed.

"Well, that was sexy," I say to Mark as he hugs me tight.

"Anything you—"

"Oh no you don't. Don't even begin to tell me that you thought my throwing up was sexy," I say and watch him laugh.

"Yeah, I guess you're right," he says grinning. "But honestly—"

"Stop. Lets just not talk about it," I say and pull him with me back to Gio and the others.

"Clean up on aisle nine," Tom says smiling.

I can feel myself turn red. I turn toward Gregor and say, "Sorry about that. I actually do need to clean—"

"Oh don't even worry about it; I'll take care of it," Gregor says as if it's ridiculous that I should even mention it. "It'll give me a chance to test some of my solutions out on your specific organic compounds."

"My organic compounds?"

"Of course. There has to be something in your chemical makeup that was released when you healed Gio."

"You have a healing ability, Jo," Tom says excitedly. "Now that's cool."

"The problem was, though, when you healed her, something foreign must have been released that caused your body to react to its presence, appropriately, though. Expelling the antigen in that manner is by far the quickest and most efficient way to do that," he says seemingly impressing with my ability to barf.

"Why would her body create something that it couldn't handle?" Sandy asks sounding concerned.

"It must have something to do with her remarkable healing ability. Do you have any insights?" Gregor asks Guida.

"I have many insights, Gregor, as do you. None of which will ever give us the answers regarding the evolution of the one true source—Jo."

Tom begins to say something then stops himself. All I can think is he must have tons of respect for Guida because whatever sarcastic comment was about to come out of his mouth, he did something he never does. He showed restraint.

Gregor, in obvious awe, of Guida asks, "This foresight into her behavior, is it telepathic?"

"Oh wow, can we stay focused? No need to start the loopy conversations just yet," Tom says wide eyed at Gregor.

"Oh, right," Gregor says, smiling at Tom.

As the monitor continues its steady rhythm, Gregor grabs a syringe from a box lying on the table.

"She stable right now," he says inserting a needle into her arm. "I'm giving her something so she'll rest while she heals."

"How's Gio?" Harrison asks, interrupting my thoughts. I fill him in on everything in our own special way, and after reiterating it out loud, I see Ava hug him. God those two are so cute.

Sandy and I lock eyes for a moment, and I can tell he's thankful to me for helping her, even though I really didn't have a choice in the matter ... not a conscious one anyway. At that moment, all I want is to reiterate to him that she's going to be fine, or at the very least give him a celebratory hug, but I can't. Mark could read into my intentions.

Gregor looks at me as if I were some new substance or something. "I have to run tests, but this is—"

"She's not a science experiment," Mark says suddenly, interrupting Gregor's valuation of me.

Harrison starts to walk over to us with Ava and the new girl following right behind. I get the sense he's trying to head off something between Mark and his father. When they were all together earlier, did Mark finally get a chance to clear the air? I hope so, for Mark's sake.

"No, of course not," Gregor says, but I can tell the scientist in him is still stoked. "It's just, she was again able to do something I honestly didn't think was feasible for our kind."

"Your science reveals her truths, yet you still compare her to others," Guida says cryptically.

"My truths?" I ask, trying to decipher her words. They're talking about me as if I'm not here.

"She means your abilities," Tom says, acknowledging more than my question.

Gregor, his head still in the science of it all, asks, "But are they not connected?"

"Connected but not comparable. Not to her, for she is—"

Oh, god. Don't say special or, worse, chosen, I think right before Guida looks at me oddly, then continues.

"As you and the others will continue to evolve after the branding to your own specific abilities, Jo is evolving on a different level ... one I have no prevision of."

"Wait ... what did you just say?" Tom asks. I steal a glance at Mark and realize he picked up on it, too.

Ignoring Tom's question, Gregor says, "But even without precognition within the scope of her development, aren't her abilities still measurable?"

"Measurable by you ... yes."

"By me, specifically?"

"As you've seen, your science is and will be essential throughout Jo's evolution."

"Meaning the evolution of her abilities?"

"In many words."

"In so many words," Tom interjects.

Guida nods.

"I'm afraid the degree to which I was able to replicate her energy source was the limit of my capabilities. That project was one I was working on for months in the tower lab. I mean, without the proper resources, time ... it just isn't feasible that I could—"

"You doubt your own truths," Guida says interrupting Gregor's uncharacteristic ranting.

"No, it's just, as she evolves any other abilities she may possess would require scientific analysis. Studying the effects alone would require..."

Gregor, throwing his hands in the air, shakes his head as if perplexed.

Tom decides he's seen enough. "For god sakes, Gregor, did you not pick up on the fact that you're getting your own ticket to the save-the-world show? I mean, shit, it doesn't take my incredible intuition to figure that your part in all this will probably be the go-to science geek."

"He's right, I've seen it," Harrison says, with him and the others now standing among us. Ava loops her arm in mine solemnly. The emotional turmoil her small frame has dealt with lately showing as she leans against me.

"Why didn't you say anything?" Tom asks.

"It was earlier. When Gio was, uh ... well, it was just a flash, not even a vision really."

"Oh, that's why you got that strange look on your face," Ava says.

Harrison's in my head then. "Jo, Mark's not going to—"

"This is ridiculous," Mark says suddenly to Harrison. "I mean, I get it. Everything you told me is real, and honestly, none of it surprises me, it really doesn't. But I refuse to believe he's supposed to be such an integral part of it," Mark says scoffing as he glances at Gregor.

So Harrison did talk with Mark after Ava sent him here.

"I'm staying out of this," Tom says to no one in particular.

"Son, there are things we need to discuss, and we will, but not right now," Gregor says.

"Hey, at least you're consistent," Mark says snidely.

As I glance around, I realize I've branded every person I see here right now except Mark and Gregor. I would never want Mark to feel excluded in any way, not from everything that's happening with the branding and all, but especially not from me. But if things move ahead in the way Guida and Harrison say they will, Mark will again be reminded how different he is and not just because he doesn't carry the unusual DNA strands. No, because of the choices I keep involuntarily making.

"He knows ... he'd never blame you for anything,"

Harrison says to me only then.

I smile at him but doubt his words.

The new girl takes her eyes off Guida and I for a second; even she isn't oblivious to the tension between Mark and his father. Knowing about the twelve and no telling what else, I wonder what she thinks as she looks around the room at the people that I've chosen so far to be part of this team of saviors.

"So now that you've informed us that Jo is going to brand Gregor, does she just grab him or what," Tom asks Guida.

"I know not what she will do," Guida says as if asking her was ridiculous.

"That's helpful," Tom says sarcastically.

It's amazing how everyone else seems to be either in awe of Guida or too freaked out to pay her much attention, but not Tom. After his momentary lapse in the cave, he seems to have fallen back to his usual brusqueness. I guess the novelty of interacting with a person from another planet has already worn off for him.

"The branding must be an energy-based reaction to a catalyst within your thought process," Gregor says to me as if trying to find a scientific approach to this craziness.

"Hey Jo, if you want to shut him up, you know branding him right now would be an option," Tom says and I can't help but smile at the way these two interact. I couldn't imagine two people more opposite. Tom's intuition offset by Gregor's science based practicality.

As I contemplate this, it hits me. What's the most practical way I could brand someone?

Tuning everyone out, I concentrate on Gregor and the things that make him remarkable while at the same time I move toward him to place my hand on his chest. Wondering if this approach will work, I get my answer within seconds.

Gregor's reaction validates the violent assault on his body as the vision fills my consciousness.

14

For all of Tom's frustration with Gregor, I can't tell who's more excited that he was branded, Gregor or Tom. They've been talking nonstop with Joshua since it happened a few minutes ago.

Even though I knowingly triggered this branding, it was mostly instinctual. My sense of control was thwarted as my body became reactive once the branding kicked in. This lack of control over my abilities and even my actions is what probably has Guida here in the first place. To make sure that I brand everyone and build the team that's supposed to save her world. If my worlds' future existence was in the hands of an evolving teenager, I'd be checking in too.

As Sandy, Ava, and Harrison check on Gio, the new girl speaks with Guida. I should probably be interested in that particular conversation, but my attention turns back to Mark. With everything that's happened, I would do anything just to get a moment alone with him.

He notices me coming, and by the look on his face, I can tell he must be hoping the same thing.

"What happened when you were transported?" I ask. "You came here?"

"Jo, I thought I was going to go out of my mind being separated from you again. Yes, I was here, but I didn't know where here even was."

"God, I'm so sorry. I wish—"

"I think it's time we were all introduced to your new friend," Tom says, walking up with the others and breaking our moment as he motions toward the new girl.

Although she stays back, her gaze suggests a keen interest in us. She's now a part of this growing team but probably still feels very much like an outsider.

"She's the one that was following us ... the one with the black car," Sandy says, thankfully taking the pressure of Tom and his thousand possible questions.

If Tom's surprised, he doesn't let on. Instead he says, "I think it's about time we all sat down for a powwow?"

"I completely agree," Sandy says and I can tell he's wanting answers, too.

We go over to a long metal table resting up against a large cabinet filled with all sorts of unusual objects. Just looking at these things with their sharp edges and coiled metal workings makes me wonder what else Gregor has created.

"What's that for?" Ava asks.

Following her gaze, I notice some long cylinder-looking thing. It's like a weird-looking tanning bed.

"That was one of the preliminary instruments I used when trying to replicate Jo's energy potential. Of course, I only had the meteorite at the time," Gregor says as if it were the most normal thing in the world.

I wonder then how many crazy tests have been done here and in the lab at Pym Tower just to find out more about me and what I can do. How many people were hurt to uncover those secrets?

I feel a wave of guilt as various hypothetical images of torture enter my thoughts.

"You're not to blame for anything that went on here or that other place Jo. How could you be? Besides, what you did for Gio, that was incredible," I hear Harrison say suddenly in my head. His words, so poignant and seemingly indisputable, change my thinking instantly. How connected are we?

Tom clears his throat then begins to speak as if he were running a board meeting. "First off, we don't have much time but there are some things we need discuss before we have to deal with Mitchell. I mean, the asshole's still out there."

"Aren't we safe as long as we're here?" Ava asks.

Tom takes a minute to choose his words. She seems to be the only one he does that for.

"Probably, but if there's one thing I've learned, it's not to underestimate him. So I just want to play it safe, that's all," he says and smiles reassuringly at her.

"So what's your plan?" Sandy asks with a hint of attitude. I guess they still have some things to work out.

"With all the shit that's happened over the last few days, I just feel like we need to get a handle on it all. Figure out what we know and what we need to know. Like for instance ... who the hell are you?" he asks looking right at the new girl.

She challenges his gaze, and I can't tell if she's about to attack him or bow. He notices and is instantly enthralled. Of course, someone else for him to figure out.

"I branded her," I say hoping to relieve the tension.

It takes him a minute of sizing her up before he says, "I figured ... can I see it?"

She looks at me as if questioning his motives.

"Uh, maybe we should start with names," I say. "My name is Jo and he's Tom."

Nodding her head toward me, her demeanor changes and she says, "I am Chiyoko."

The room is silent as we all stare at this young girl. It's not her peculiar physical appearance that has us speechless, but her way. Maybe it's her voice, her movements, I don't know, but whatever it is, it's dark ... edgy. Different from the rest of us.

Turning toward Tom and I, she unzips the front of her jacket. Its material is a strange blackish-green color and seems to be made of thin leather. How could she possibly fit her arsenal in there? Pulling down the front of her shirt, she shows us another of the twelve symbols branded right above her heart.

"So, you are one of us," he says checking her out as if she were some new hot rod that just came off the assembly line.

"Can I ask why you've been trying to kill Jo?" Sandy asks.

"I was sent to kill her," she says matter-of-factly.

"By whom?"

"By a small secret order of monks in the mountains of eastern Asia."

Tom's mouth drops open. "Well, that clears it up," he says sarcastically.

I watch as the edge of the strange tattoo coming up her neck from underneath her jacket flexes ever so slightly at Tom's attitude. It's just a minor reaction but enough to tell me she isn't used to dealing with people like him, but honestly, who is?

"So why did they send you to kill Jo?" Sandy asks point-blank not being deterred by the originality of her story.

She glances at me and I can tell she's not enjoying the inquisition.

"We just want some answers, that's all," Tom says eyeing Sandy.

"It was my final test. I was told killing Jo would begin my part in the prophecy."

"You had so many chances before the club to take me out, why didn't you?" I ask, thinking back on the multitude of times I dealt with her driving that black death-machine.

"I was told of specifics regarding the exact time I was

to kill you. For my training it was when you were at your strongest. That club and its oddities–"

"But you weren't supposed to kill her. Why would these monks tell you that you were?" Sandy asks intently.

"Their motivations are not for me to question."

"Great, and where are these monks again?" Tom asks suspiciously.

"I come from far away, a mountain retreat that's completely isolated from the outside world. I lived there with them."

"Mountain retreat huh. Then how is it that you can drive that hell on wheels the way you do? I doubt the monks are used to burning that kind of rubber," Tom says.

This is when I would expect Sandy to step in and try to defuse Tom. Instead, Sandy just stares at the girl as if he's still on the fence about her himself. I know she was trying to kill me, but doesn't the branding kind of change all that?

Most of my upbringing, my training, was with the monks. Once I was to begin my change, I came here, to be near the meteorite. Here I have continued learning but in different ways, using different weapons. The car was one."

"One that doesn't fit in that jacket of yours," Sandy says. He was hit by so many of those discs he's probably wondering what all she has in there.

She just smiles at him, somewhat menacing but then with her oddly cool canine teeth it's hard to not see her smile as anything else.

"How did you know you needed to come here?" I ask.

"It was seen. I was brought up with the belief that living in complete isolation is the only way one can truly see."

"Truly see?"

"The monks have always been known for their ability to see things, many things, and they were sought out by a person of power from this area because of it.

"Someone from this area, who?"

"That was many years ago. They never spoke of him, just of the truths that he brought."

There's that word again—truths.

"What do you mean, truths?"

"He was wanting them to use their gifts so that he may gain knowledge about things he had seen."

"What had he seen," Harrison asks probably wanting to know if this person has the same knack for having visions as he does?

"Many things, things not of Earth," she says and looks at Guida.

Guida just stands there, her eyes moving around the room in that weird alien way. She's emotionless, stoic even, but definitely taking it all in.

Chiyoko seems uncertain but just a glance at me and all her uncertainty seems to dissipate. As if everything she's been told all her life is finally validated, just by looking at me.

"The monks say he had a vision of a prophecy. A prophecy of a great battle fought on another world but that could alter the fate of ours."

She then precedes to take her jacket off. It falls to the floor with a clank. Grabbing the bottom of her shirt she rips it off over her head. She's left wearing a tight black tank stretched tight across her small, almost nonexistent breasts and tight abs. Black leathery pants made from the same material as her jacket hug the rest of her petite body. Agile-looking and as perfectly sculpted as you would expect a person to be that had been in training all their life, she stands in the center of the room and removes her tank.

We all stare in awe. Tattooed on her upper back is the symbol I branded into her skin. Now I know why she didn't look at it after I branded her. She knew what it was. Knew what it looked like. She's been looking at it for years.

"Holy shit," Tom exclaims.

I stare at the symbol and see various other tattoos dispersed around her arms, chest and neck. The cave, some odd-looking weapons, a strange landscape scene, and even a dark menacing figure of sorts fading into a blacked-out portion of her skin. That's when something deep inside tells me not to dwell on the figure, to move on to something else instead.

I do, and notice eyes, strange and alien, eyes that look exactly like mine and Guida's. They are resting just above her breasts as if looking back at me, validating everything she has said until now. Now I know why she was staring at Guida and me so much earlier. It's one thing to hear strange stories, but to actually see things for yourself, unfolding right before you ... that has to shake anyone to their core.

Although it takes everyone a minute to digest the boldness of this girl, half-naked and showing a room full of strangers her body art, Tom, as usual, gets there faster.

"It's all connected. The things Harrison told us ... what we already knew. It connects perfectly."

"Yes, and the timeline's right," Gregor agrees.

"What are you talking about," Sandy asks.

"The he she referred to. The person that had the vision of those," Tom says motioning towards Chyoko and her tattoos.

"He was one of the original board members working with Irina. I remember when he went away for a while. Could never figure out where, but right after is when The Order started. That's also when I found out about the twelve symbols and etched them on a metal circle to be used as a piece of decor in your cabin. You see, the symbols, he was obsessed with them. Until lately, I never knew why."

"A team of twelve," Harrison mutters in my head.

"That's also when they recruited, well ... took Gregor."

Mark looks at Gregor, shocked by the revelation. So Gregor didn't just abandon him. No, it was The Order and their uncanny way of destroying families.

"How was he able to have the vision so long ago," Gregor asks, oblivious to the effect the recent information is having on his son. "Harrison didn't begin having visions until Jo went through her change."

"He is a seer, like Harrison ... like Guida," Guida says confusing everyone for a moment.

"He was a seer," Tom mumbles sarcastically, giving the impression that the man that sought out the monks so long ago is no longer.

"At the time of Jo's birth every seer had a vision of the prophecy," Harrison says then looks at Guida surprised to have said it.

"So do all seers see the same visions," Gregor asks seemingly very interested in Harrison and Guida's telepathic abilities.

"No, we are not the same. Harrison was chosen. He will evolve until he is like no other," Guida says.

"Like no other? Is that even a legitimate way of describing someone," Harrison says in my head causing me to chuckle and then everyone to glance at me. I've really have to get a handle on this telepathy thing before everyone thinks the chosen one is off her rocker.

"What about you? How do you see things," Ava asks Guida.

"She is the most evolved on her planet," Harrison says being prodded by Guida again. "When Jo was born she saw the prophecy, uh ... like big scale ... not really sure. Uh, I think what she means is she saw a more big universal view of it. Yes, right. She saw the prophecy as a change in destiny for many worlds."

"Wow, that's amazing," Ava says smiling at Guida.

"This is how I came to be here ... to help guide you and those you have chosen," Guida says to me specifically.

Choyoko reaches up and touches her brand causing me wonder how much of a say I actually have in all this choosing business. It's supposed to be my choices that guide the prophecy or something like that, but I still find it hard to believe I would choose Choyoko, no matter how cool she looks.

"So how did you end up with the monks and involved in all this Choyoko," Harrison asks deciding to be proactive and find an answer to my question instead of sitting around pondering it.

"You may all call me Chi," she says pulling her shirt back on. "The man from your area had seen that I, a young orphaned girl of nine, would come to them. I would come to them not only to learn their ways but to gain knowledge and, most importantly, to train."

"Train," I ask, suddenly enthralled. Looking around at the others, I realize I'm not the only one.

"Train to fight."

"Fight?"

"Yes, they are spiritual in the way they live and the way they fight. They have taught me how to fight in a way that has prepared me physically and mentally."

"For the prophecy?" Tom asks skeptically.

Looking directly at me, she says, "For Jo. So she may fulfill the prophecy. It's the reason for my training, ultimately the reason for my very existence."

"What?" Mark says.

I can't believe what I've just heard. "You believe you exist only to help me fulfill this prophecy thing."

"Ultimately, yes."

I try to wrap my head around it. It's crazy ... insane. This is the real world. People can't go around believing that they need to make that kind of difference.

"So what exactly is the prophecy?" Mark asks.

"Jo picks eleven of us to go with her on a world saving journey to her planet," Tom says nodding towards Guida. "Once there it's up to us or more likely Jo, to do something I can only assume will be quite amazing that will hopefully change our fate of being obliterated."

So there it is, so simple, yet so terrifying.

Mark looks stunned. No one says a word as I think for the first time it's all starting to sink in. Guida, the prophecy. I'm sure a few months ago if I'd have asked anyone other than Chi about all this, they'd have thought I was out of my mind, but here we are.

A little later, while everyone's still mulling over everything that was discussed, I decide I need a distraction from my own thoughts and start to scope out this lab of Gregor's. This place is like Tony Stark meets Dr. Frankenstein. It has the same practicality as the lab in the Pym Tower but without the flash. With all the various equipment strewn about, I can't help but wonder how he keeps all his experiments organized. All I see is a hodgepodge of workstations with impressively complicated-looking contraptions. It's like getting a glimpse into the intricate workings of his mind.

That's when I notice the back corner of the large room is partitioned off by a gray metal wall.

"You're looking at Joshua's domain behind there," Tom

says, well aware that I'm taking everything in. I thought he was talking with Chi. Does the man not miss anything?

"When I was transported into that cave, he's the reason all the chips fell into place when taking down The Order. Let's just say he basically runs the show when Gregor and I aren't around. Keeps the show running anyway," he says smirking to himself.

"I sure do," Joshua says as he comes up holding a tablet. Handing it to Tom, he says, "You both gotta see what the security feed picked up from the club."

Tom and Gregor hover over the electronic device as Joshua's gaze drifts over Guida and I.

"I'm what you'd call the James Bond of cryptographic systems," he says and winks at me as if I'm supposed to be impressed. "I've yet to come across a system that is absolutely secure," he says snickering.

"Really?" I say.

"Yeah, he can do some amazing things," Sandy says, and I can tell he's actually being sincere. Joshua just beams.

"Speaking of amazing things. Looks as though you're able to do a little more with your blasting ability than we thought," Tom says handing the tablet back to Joshua as he eyes me curiously.

So that's what they were looking at over at the club, not Chi—me.

"What do you mean?" Mark asks with an edge to his voice. I bet he's getting sick of being the last person to hear about the things his girlfriend can or will do.

"Look for yourself," Tom saying motioning for Joshua to show him.

Joshua pushes a few buttons before handing it to Mark. A video from inside the club begins playing as Joshua kicks into tour guide mode again.

"You see, we monitor the inside of the club as well as the surrounding areas," Joshua says to the others as Mark stares intensely at the screen. "So I was able to go back and figure out what happened when the glitch occurred."

"Glitch?" Sandy asks.

"Yeah, there was a strange power surge when you guys were over there that caused a few of my systems to overload and cut out. I mean, the kind of power it would take to do that ... well, it just shouldn't be possible," Joshua says. "Anyway, I was able to look on the security mainframe to find the cause."

"Yeah, like you knocking an entire club of people out cold," Tom says eyeing me.

Mark hands the tablet back to Joshua then glances at Sandy. Did he see Sandy do something on the video?

"The energy source from within her. She does have complete control over it then," Gregor says to no one specifically, as if he's having a eureka moment.

"That's what I'm thinking," Tom says probably running through all the scenarios of what this could mean for his big picture.

Gregor acts as if he finds the whole idea unbelievable. "I've become familiar with the type of energy she emits, duplicated it even, but I wasn't sure of its scope. But if she's, in fact, able to not only harness this energy but control it, well ... that changes its ramifications completely."

"How so?" Tom asks.

"Like the situation over in the club. The heart is electrical, so it would be possible for someone with her ability to give it just enough of a jolt to induce a temporary cardiogenic syncope."

"English please," Tom says irritably.

"What I'm saying is, since Jo is able to control the power, then she could shock someone just enough to knock them out—normal people at least."

But if that's true, what about the fact that Mitchell told that creepy kidnapper guy that my "mojo," as he called it, didn't work on normal people? Was Mitchell just lying or does he really not know? How could he know?

"Jo, would you say it was a similar feeling to when you ... uh, blasted Mitchell?" Gregor asks enthralled.

It only takes me a few seconds to remember how I felt when I blasted Mitchell. "No, not at all, in the club I was just uh, irritated. I just needed the people to get out of my way, but with Mitchell—I wanted to kill Mitchell."

Gregor smiles. "I'm sorry, you misunderstand me. I mean, did it physically feel the same?"

Feeling like an emotional idiot, I try to think. "It felt the same."

Tom chimes in, "It felt the same, but you were wanting two very different outcomes."

"Very."

Turning to Gregor, "Again, like I've said all along, her abilities are emotionally driven. Interesting. Scary as hell ... but interesting."

15

—

"Sandy, she's awake," Ava says suddenly from across the room.

Within seconds, we're around Gio needing no formal validation that she's almost healed. As gorgeous as always, she radiates her usual goddess-like quality. Her skin, astonishingly vibrant compared to earlier, is almost too perfect, too supple, for someone that's been through what she has. If it were anyone else, I'd be shocked to see them like this, but it's Gio, so I wouldn't expect anything less.

Gregor takes a quick look under her covering then reaches over to turn off the monitor. Now that's a good sign.

"Your sedative wore off a little quicker than I expected, but that's fine—I am already seeing synthesis of your collagen tissue," he says then smiles at me as if impressed all over again.

"Hey," she says to me, her voice shockingly strong and smooth.

"Hi."

"I had a dream about you," she says then lets her gaze rest on Mark. He seems surprised by the way she looks at him and smiles back oddly. So her interest in him hasn't changed, I see.

"I need to talk to Sandy," she says worriedly as she begins to shift on the table.

Gregor gently holds her down. "Even though your healing process has moved past your ventral cavity, you really shouldn't try to move quite yet."

"My ventral..."

"Well, that sounds fun," Tom says hurriedly. "What he

means to say is, just a little bit longer and you'll be good as new. That is, thanks to Jo here for saving your life."

She seems shocked for a moment as she deciphers his words.

"You saved my ... and I was beginning to think that being around you was bad for my health."

All I can muster is a weak smile as images of her being sliced in the head with a saw in the high school shop class and the two discs lodging themselves into her skull in the alley earlier flash through my mind. She definitely has a point.

"Not just that ... Jo branded you," Ava says excitedly as she comes to the side of the table and takes Gio's hand. Gio's face instantly lights up upon seeing Ava's huge grin.

"We were so worried. I don't think I've ever cried so much ... but now, it's better than we could have imagined. You're one of us ... one of the twelve," Ava says then gently exposes Gio's brand.

"The twelve," Gio asks as she runs her fingers over the raised flesh. Her gaze finds me, and I can't help but feel like she's learning what she thought was a strange dream wasn't a dream at all. I think back to the vision we had and wonder if that could be it. Does she remember it ... or the way it would have made her feel? Did she see that she's the one I'll need to keep me focused, sharp ... alive...

Sandy steps forward. "You know, you really gave us a scare back there."

Gio makes another effort to sit up, but Gregor clears his throat as a reminder to stay still. Exasperated, she says to Sandy, "I need to talk to you, I need to explain why I did those things–"

"Hey you have nothing to explain," Sandy says and I can tell he means it.

"Actually she does. I need to know what happened out there," Tom says.

"Tom, is this really a good time?" Sandy asks.

"No, it's fine ... I'm fine," Gio says then seems to go off for a moment with her thoughts.

"We missed them somehow," she says as if trying to wrap her head around the idea that she had messed up. "We swept the area before going down to the perimeter boundary to wait for the device to put them down. There wasn't anyone there. Sandy, I was sure of it," she says looking right at Sandy now. She knows if anyone believes her, it would be him.

"Then what happened?" Tom asks.

Gio thinks for a moment, then continues. "It was only seconds before they were there, all around us. It was Mitchell and his men. They were all so fast, so ... precise. Like mini-execution teams. They grabbed us and killed all four of them in exactly the same way at exactly the same time," Gio says as if in shock at how smoothly it went.

"What about you?" Tom asks.

Her memory seems to kick in and she takes a shaky deep breath.

"There was nothing I could do to save them ... nothing. I felt the stick when they grabbed me, and I couldn't move. I could see everything. I could see the others burn, die, but I couldn't do anything to help them. It was as if my body was paralyzed, but I could still see and feel everything. I felt it when they shoved that thing inside me but ... but that was nothing compared..."

She glances at Sandy and seems unsure. Maybe she knows he'll blame himself, or maybe she's just embarrassed about being in that situation in the first place. It's hard to tell with Gio.

Regaining her composure a little, she continues, "Once it was inside me, they did something to it, flipped a switch, pushed a button, I don't know. All I know is I remember him saying it was on, then the noise started. That's when I felt the fire, like my insides were being burned ... it's all a little fuzzy after that," she says huskily.

Sandy puts his hand on her shoulder to calm her.

"What I don't understand is why they were there. There is no way he could have had a heads up, no way," Tom says more to himself then anyone but then suddenly seems to think of something.

"Gio, did you actually see Mitchell?"

She thinks for a moment then realization runs across her and Sandy's face when she answers: "No."

"That bastard," Tom says. "He knew. I don't know how, but he knew. The question now is, how much more does he know?"

"This should do it," Gregor says as he swiftly inserts a needle into Gio's arm. She flinches then the clear liquid disappears. "A little more sedative to take the edge off."

"More sedative," she asks as her eyes begin to get heavy. A few seconds later and she's asleep again. Tom and Sandy look instantly relieved.

"So what does this guy want?" Mark asks.

"Power ... control. Honestly, I really don't know what the guy wants. What I do know is he believes our kind," Tom says, motioning to everyone in the room other than Mark, "are better than, well ... you."

Mark's eyes dart toward me for a second. He's pissed.

Tom seems aware but continues anyway. "That's why Irina recruited him. He's had no qualms about anything she's asked him to do. I guess somewhere along the line his own agenda kicked in. Now I'm sure he wants to find this place and get his hands on whatever Gregor has here and probably some of us. The asshole has goals, what can I say."

"I know he wants to get his hands on me," I say, but

when I see Mark's reaction I instantly regret it.

"Yeah, but you aren't his only motivation," Tom says matter-of-factly. "He wants power and so that means he wants information. When dealing with all this scientific shit, information is power, and frankly ... he wants it all."

"You mean computer files?" I ask wondering if that was the main reason Tom had Joshua destroy all these computers with a virus.

Tom smiles. "No, the information he wants, the only information that matters at the end of the day, is in your dad's head," he says looking at Mark.

"If he can get to Gregor, control him, then he probably thinks the sky's the limit. With Gregor on his side, he figures he can do just about anything. Maybe even do away with Jo."

Tom looks right at me then.

"I know the bastard and I know nothing on this earth would bring him more satisfaction right now than killing you."

His words hit home and my heart sinks.

Sandy stares down at Gio with an odd expression on his face. What's he thinking? Is he realizing now the task he's taken on by having to protect me?

Turning to Gregor, he suddenly seems to think of something. "When you were attempting to take the device out, you ran into a problem, said that something in it was causing a problem with the device itself. Could Mitchell have been able to understand the science involved enough to alter the device?"

"I doubt the technical aspect of it is his forte," Gregor says.

"Yeah, but I wouldn't put it past him to come up with the idea," Tom interjects.

"What if the device malfunctioning in Gio wasn't a

typical fluke?" Sandy asks.

"Yeah, exactly. What if it really wasn't a problem with the mechanism at all? What if it was planned? What if, like Sandy's getting at, the device was altered in some way?" Tom asks.

"I just don't think he'd have the technical knowledge. Most of the tests we ran early on were unsuccessful partly because the device proved to be too unstable. Ms. Welch herself said it was glitchy," Gregor says then seems to suddenly realize something.

"Oh, shit," Tom says quickly understanding exactly what Gregor is thinking.

"What is it?" Sandy asks.

"Exactly what you were getting at. Mitchell altered the fucking device. He may have gotten a science geek—no offense, Gregor—like Ms. Welch to do the technical work, but the concept, I'm telling you ... it's all his."

"Who's Ms. Welch?" I ask.

"The sexy redhead you saw passed out in the lab," Tom says as if liking whatever image just popped into his head. "She was Irina and Gregor's assistant, so I guess you could say she had both hands in the cookie jar. Definitely someone Mitchell would want to get to."

I remember the woman lying on the lab floor. Dressed in a crisp white lab coat over a pair of dark-colored dress pants. Heels on her feet that seemed surprisingly high for a scientist. Her soft-looking shiny red hair splayed on the hard floor. I remember how Gio seemed to have it out for her, and I especially remember what Tom said he had done to her.

"That damn Mitchell," Tom says. "I have to say he's one of the few people on this planet that can still surprise me from time to time. I mean, I knew he was plotting against Irina, I just didn't realize how thorough his little coup was.

To get someone like Ms. Welch, the one person that's not only close to the boss but involved in the science, in on your plan ... brilliant," he says staring at the device.

"That still doesn't quite explain why Mitchell tampered with the device," Gregor says.

"He had to have known we'd bring Gio to you and that you'd try to get the damn thing out of her. Probably even knew you'd figure out he altered it and look at it closely. He wanted it right where it was, inside Gio and inside ... oh shit, this warehouse."

Gregor suddenly grabs the device off the table and heads to another part of the warehouse calling out for Joshua as he goes. Whatever Tom is getting at, Gregor understands.

Tom seems almost in disbelief as he says, "Mitchell ... you are one slick motherfucker."

"What is it?" I ask, not completely getting it but feeling the urgency?

"Tom thinks Mitchell planted a tracker inside the device," Sandy says to me hurriedly.

"Then we need to get Jo out of here," Mark says gently grabbing my arm protectively.

"Exactly," Sandy says as if that's the only thing on his mind, too. "Tom, I think the cabin's best."

"Yeah, there's no way he'd know about that place ... no way. I'm thinking Ava," Tom says to Sandy.

My mind connects the dots when I hear them say her name. They want Ava to beam me over to the cabin.

"I can send her over now," Ava says stepping forward as if happy to help.

Panicky, I turn my chest away from her and stammer, "I'm not leaving everyone—"

"It's definitely a tracking device of some sort, seems to be remote activated," Gregor says coming up to us suddenly holding a section of the device.

"Has it been turned on yet?"

"I'm afraid it has, and I have no way of knowing how long it's been tracking."

"Shit, we led the bastard right here ... damn!"

For a second, no one says anything. Glancing around the room, my heart sinks. Even with Chi and Sandy to help fight him and his cronies, I know Mitchell ... he'll hit us where it hurts me the most.

"Buddy, I think now would be a great time to impress me with some of your security and weapons shit, cause I know you got some tricks up your sleeve," Tom says to Gregor.

Gregor nods, seemingly not rattled in any way. "Joshua I need you to–"

"Already on it boss ... one data flush coming up," Joshua says running toward his partitioned area.

"Don't lock down systems until I get the scanner up and running," Gregor yells out after him as he quickly sets the device down beside Tom.

Tom walks over to a part of the wall adorned with levers and buttons, something right out of one of those underground military bunkers you see in the movies where the men that control the nukes are housed.

"The one thing Mitchell relies heavily on, too heavily if you ask me, is guns," Gregor says walking over and pulling the lever. A heavy steel door suddenly comes slamming down in front of one of only two doors in the whole warehouse.

Gregor pushes the last button on the right causing a loud whirring noise to begin on the other side of the warehouse, where the other entrance is.

"What the hell?" Tom says.

"The technology is based on MRI scanners."

"You mean those big things people lay in to get their head scanned or whatever?" Tom asks.

"Exactly. They magnetize the mechanisms in weapons, which can alter the functionality of the weapon or render it completely useless altogether. In this case it depends on the velocity with which the person walks through the scanner, or uh ... the front door. I've altered the delivery system to localize the device to the entry point and weakened the magnetic fields so the person moving through it won't realize their weapon's been affected until they go to use it."

"Brilliant. Magnetize the weapons so any numb-nut that brings a weapon through the front door is affected ... now that's going to be fun to watch," Tom says.

Alarms suddenly start to blare throughout the building. Even Gregor seems surprised until they stop.

"Uh, my bad," Joshua yells out.

Sandy glances at me then turns to Tom. "I think we should send–"

There's suddenly a loud clunk then the lights go out.

"That's not me," Joshua yells out as we all stand in complete darkness.

A second later and different, much dimmer lights illuminate the room.

"The backup generator lights," Gregor says. "They're on a five-second delay–"

We're cast in darkness again as the generator lights abruptly go out.

"That can't be good," Tom says.

"The security has a three-part lighting system built in. Three more seconds and..."

Suddenly small round lights lining the edge of the ceiling come to life casting the warehouse in a dim yellowish hue.

"Okay, this sucks," Tom says and I don't know if he means the lights or the situation altogether.

"What about Gio?" Sandy asks.

"Yeah, in her condition, could she handle Ava sending her to the cabin?" Tom asks Gregor.

"I wouldn't risk it."

The device suddenly makes a slight clicking sound.

"What the hell was that?" Tom asks.

Gregor looks closely at the device as if to inspect it, but before he can even touch it, it starts beeping loudly. He looks up at Tom. "Everyone get back!"

Sandy lunges for the device and scoops it up. "Where do I go?" he asks Gregor.

Mark instantly starts to move Chi, Harrison, Ava, Guida, and me toward the other side of the warehouse. I feel so help-less as I'm herded with the others in an attempt to get us out of harm's way.

The beeping beeps faster, jolting my already frayed nerves.

Mark responds by putting himself between me and the device. "I'm absolutely not letting you–"

Suddenly, from across the room there's an intense flash of light just as a mind-numbing boom shocks my senses.

For a few seconds, I just stand there unable to move. Unable to understand what just happened.

"Oh my god," I hear Mark say right before he takes off in the direction of the others. I come to my senses quickly and am right behind.

I see him then. Sandy, on his back, is lying on the floor with his eyes squeezed shut trying to catch his breath.

"My eyes are stinging so bad," Joshua, sitting on the floor shrieks, as he cradles his eyes in the palms of his hands.

Mark runs over to Gregor as I fall to my knees beside Sandy. I'm unable to speak, unable to even ask him if he's okay as I watch fresh bloodstains rapidly appear among the old ones on his shirt.

"Sandy's hurt," I hear myself yell as I look around the room.

Ava helps Tom sit up.

"What's wrong with him?" Tom asks as he rubs his ears. His eyes are watering.

"Looks like shrapnel of some sort from the grenade," Mark says bending down beside me as he looks under Sandy's shirt.

Grenade. The device was tracking us but was also a bomb, or grenade or whatever. As I try to wrap my head around Mitchell's purpose, Sandy tries to sit up.

"Sandy you're hurt," I hear myself say shakily.

"I'm fine," Sandy says grunting.

"Oh wow, I'm finally starting to see something again," Joshua says relief apparent in his voice. "What was that?"

"Some type of flash or stun grenade," Gregor says, being helped up by Harrison and Chi. "They're intended to disorient with blinding flashes of light and deafening sounds," he continues as he walks over to Gio.

"Yeah, I got that," Tom says sarcastically.

Sandy lifts his shirt, then lets out a deep breath before reaching down and ripping one of the metal objects out of his body. It falls to the floor with a ping.

"How's Gio?" he asks.

"She's fine," Gregor says picking up the metal piece Sandy threw on the floor. "A flash grenade with shrapnel."

"Do you have anything we could use to help him take these out?" Mark asks.

"Come on," Gregor says. "I have some tweezers over here somewhere." Gregor takes Mark to retrieve them.

With Mark gone, my guard instantly comes down.

"It hasn't been a good night for you and sharp objects," I say not making eye contact and trying to sound normal even as my voice quivers.

He gives me a sweet smile before trying to lighten the mood. "Yeah, and I think my poor shirt has gotten the brunt of it."

I smile back then turn away as Mark comes up with the tweezers to help him pull out the rest of the shrapnel.

"Thanks," Sandy says to Mark as he gets to his feet. "It's already healing."

"Yeah, guess you'll be all healed in a few minutes then," Mark says, an edge to his voice.

Even though I keep forgetting how different Mark is than the rest of us, he doesn't forget. How could he when every second there's something happening to remind him?

"So that was his play," Tom says out loud to no one in particular as he paces the floor. "A flash grenade?"

"A distraction," Sandy says.

"Yeah, but from what?" Tom asks and barely has the words out before we all of a sudden hear a crash come from the main entrance hallway.

16

—

"AVA! AVA..."

Tom's trying to get her attention but she's scared. Frozen, she just stares at the entrance to the room, dreading the fact that at any moment Mitchell could come through. Harrison reacts to Tom's urgency by reaching out and grabbing Ava's shoulder.

Suddenly a canister slides across the floor, coming to a rest precisely in the middle of the room. Within a second, smoke is pouring out of it.

"Ava, hurry—send everyone to the cabin," Tom yells at her through her fogged state.

Quickly glancing at Harrison, it's as if something about his presence, touch, I don't know ... makes her respond. She spins around, and as I hear him protest in my head, she shoves her hand in his chest. He's gone.

She's seemingly surprised at what she just did. It was as if her instinct was to protect him first yet again. This time, though, it's a testament to her feelings for him. At least that's one thing I can be happy about.

She lunges toward Chi, but having just seen what Ava did to Harrison, Chi's not having any of it. She does a quick spin move, ending up completely out of Ava's reach.

Coughing, I start to feel the affects of the smoke right before I hear what sounds like a large fan being turned on. Joshua, standing in front of a large gray panel on the wall, is staring up at the ceiling as the smoke quickly begins to dissipate through a long narrow slit in the roof.

A ventilation system. Of course Gregor would have one.

With smoke lingering in the air, a black cylinder moves across the floor then in the same manner as the object that released the smoke.

"Oh shit. Everybody back, it's another—" I hear Tom yell just before I fall to the ground.

Larger and more powerful than the previous grenade, it sends a shockwave through my senses. With my eyes instinctively closed, I grab at my ears, hoping to stop the intense ringing pulsating throughout my head.

That's when I feel the vibrations of footfalls swarming into the room from the main entrance. Glancing up, I'm surprised to find that my eyes have not been affected by the blast.

In the dim illumination, I watch as Mitchell's men stream in the door.

Dressed in all black and wearing goggles, each one carries a large black gun, like the kind you'd see in a military movie. Adding to the cinematic similarities, each weapon has a laser sight attached.

The ringing, having become just a dull buzz at this point, isn't a distraction any longer. Looking over, I see Ava is rubbing her eyes, but otherwise she seems to be fine. Remembering the effects the last grenade had on Sandy, I wonder with horror if Mitchell had tweaked this grenade, too?

Jumping up, I frantically look around the room. Everything's so chaotic ... so surreal. All I can do is watch the scene unfold. Watch as everyone I care about suffers.

Spotting Mark across the room, relief courses through me and I feel like I can breathe again. He isn't hurt.

One of the guys at the door yells, "Nobody move!"

A second later he goes on to instruct everyone to freeze yet again, while the other ops guys position a laser sight on what seems like every person in the room.

Seeing the red dot positioned right over Mark's chest causes my heart rate to jump. He's the only person in the room that could actually be killed by a bullet.

Seeing all the men, all the guns, I can't react. Everything I've ever done has been driven by the force of my emotions. I've never been trained, never learned to fight. I've only been able to rely on my impulses at best, unable to predict what I would do.

Even if Gregor's scanner did work by affecting their guns in some way, would I still be able to save him from all these men? Is it a risk I could even take?

The ops guy who yelled at us starts looking around the room for something. The intense way he looks over me instantly makes me avert my eyes. If there's one person I can guarantee they want to find ... it's me.

"Objectives two and three, sector one ... confirm and tag," he says loudly to his men.

Quickly, I try to decode the jargon the man just barked to the others as I hear the guns making revving sounds. It's as if they are charging up or something. Gio, still sedated and completely unaware that a gun is pointed right at her, lies on the table with Sandy standing right next to her. Suddenly the laser-sight positioned on them changes from red to green.

My pulse quickens. The desperation I feel to change the situation is making me feel restless, antsy. I'm fast, but could I be fast enough? What about my energy blast thing?

As if reading my thoughts, the guy shouts out, "Any movement and we kill everyone!" Joshua, standing beside Tom and Gregor, immediately holds his hands up.

Tom just smirks at the guy. "So where's your boss? You know, the big guy that must have sent your ass in here first to test out all the traps and shit we have set up before coming in himself."

Although the guy seems unfazed by Tom's questioning, I see a couple of other guys look his way. It's so Tom to try to mess with someone's head even when they have a gun pointed at him.

"Objective one, sector two ... confirm and tag," the guy says emotionless.

The red laser light resting on Tom's chest quickly turns green. Tom looks down noticing the light. "I sure hope your scanners worked," he says in a low voice to Gregor.

The ops guy calling out the crazy military lingo glances around the room. His gaze rests on Mark for a few seconds, then back over to the other side of the room to Ava, Chi, Guida, and me. He's obviously the leader of this group, trying to match a code name with a face. But what about Chi? He has to wonder who she is.

"Engage sector five. Confirm priority one, two, random and possible Medusa."

Four ops guys head toward us.

"Engage sector one. Possible priority three or Medusa's bitch," the leader guy says continuing his inventory.

I see two guys advance on Mark. My mind begins to race. My fear keeps me frozen in place. With the four approaching us, Chi immediately places herself between me and the approaching threat.

"Don't move," the guy yells at Chi, now raising his gun and pointing it at her.

My nerves frayed with this temporary stalemate, I glance over at Mark. He's going to try to do something, I just know it. I can tell by the way he's obviously sizing up his aggressors and, to my horror, realizing that they're nowhere near as big as he is.

Validating my fears, he suddenly lunges at one of the men, causing the leader guy to swing his gun around. Before he can take aim, his head is thrown to the side. Blood begins to pour down and around the edges of the disc now protruding from it.

Chi's fast. So fast the two men standing in front of her don't have time to react. Grabbing the barrel of the first gun, she yanks it forward then elbow strikes the guy in the throat. The strike is precise, practiced, something meant to damage. His body convulses and before he can fall to the ground she's already pulling her spears out of the next guy.

The room erupts then, a flurry of movement, violence. Sandy, using a fighting skill set I didn't know he even possessed, repositions himself and Gio quickly.

The two other guys fire after Chi as she takes off toward the others, but their aim zigs and zags. Their guns have been altered.

So the scanner did work.

This not only irritates them but distracts them as well. Unable to lock onto Chi, they continue shooting without a thought for where she's guiding them. A second later and she's run past one of their own. They fill him with bullets.

That second delay, the small amount of time it takes for them to realize what they've done, is all she needs.

She runs toward them, then quickly alters course to the wall next to them. She's too fast, they can't follow. She jumps up, then pushes herself off the wall flying over them as she twists her body around. She lands right beside one of them, but he does nothing. He and his friend are too busy dealing with the discs that are now lodged in their heads.

Glancing over, I notice another guy pulling and pushing some mechanism on his rifle in such a way to make me think that it's jammed. A second later and Chi's made it so his jammed weapon is the least of his worries.

"Whoa buddy, good shot," Tom says sarcastically to a

guy with his gun still aimed at Tom's chest. The guy tries again, but still manages to miss him completely.

"Okay box of rocks, what you gonna do now that your manhood ain't working so good," Tom says obnoxiously.

The guy smiles menacingly at Tom then tosses his rifle to the floor and comes toward him.

"Uh, Gregor, I don't want to rush you but I think this guy's got a plan B," Tom yells to Gregor, who's managed to make his way over to one of the cabinets along the wall.

Tom stumbles off-balance as the momentum of his air punch fails to hit its target. The man scoffs and shakes his head. I hear bones crack as he rams his fist into Tom's face. A second later and the man falls to his knees. As the smoke starts to seep from his eyes and mouth, he looks at Gregor standing over him now, as if unable to understand what just happened.

Gregor, standing there holding some strange-looking silver gun, watches in amazement like a young child that just tried out his new BB gun at Christmastime.

"Now that's what I'm talking about," Tom says, wincing as he attempts to wipe some of the blood away from his nose. "What was that thing?"

" A prototype. Shoots a type of electrically charged bullets," Gregor says looking down at what is now just a smoldering crony.

"And that?"

"Oh, yeah," Gregor says tossing a sticklike thing to Joshua. He catches it easily, halting the guy about to attack him.

Joshua, cocky all of a sudden, holds up the rod in a threatening manner. It's only a second before the device reacts. Joshua yells out, dropping the rod as a jolt of electricity unexpectedly zips through his arm. Surprised, he looks between Gregor and the rod right before the guy kicks him in the gut, sending him flying against the wall behind him.

Not at all concerned about the fighting going on around him, Gregor taps his finger against his chin as if contemplating the weapon malfunction.

"That's strange. It's as if the current was stagnant. I'll have to modify the—"

"Flux capacitor, yeah we know," Tom says right before being punched in the gut by one of the two cronies taking on Gregor, Joshua, and himself simultaneously.

Grabbing Tom by the neck, the guy lifts him off his feet. He's larger than Tom, with a meaty hand that wraps easily around his throat. Tom, grabbing onto his arm, tries to pull his hand away. Suddenly, he grimaces as the blade pierces his skin. Forcefully thrown, with the precision of a pro, Chi's disc slices through the man's hand and into Tom's neck. A superficial wound for Tom, but enough to cause him momentary alarm.

Looking around the room then, I notice that most of Mitchell's team is now debilitated in some way.

Sandy and Chi fight off the last of Mitchell's men. Surprisingly in sync, their fighting abilities, ways of diverting the men's strikes, even their movements are so similar. If I didn't know better, I'd think they'd been training together for years.

My eyes lock on Mark. He's standing, safe and unharmed as one of Mitchell's team members lays on the ground a few feet away. Did he fight him off? Would he have been able to? I catch my train of thought and realize he's right. I guess I do think he's less capable than the rest of us.

I suddenly see movement at the door right before pain shoots through both my legs. Instantly, I fall to the ground as I hear Ava yell out beside me.

"Oh my god Jo, you've been shot," she exclaims bending down beside me.

"No Mark, don't move. She'll heal," I hear Sandy say. He knows as I do that if he were shot the way I was, he may never walk again.

All of a sudden the main lights come on. More of Mitchell's cronies are swarming into the room, but these men are different. Wearing different garb, yes, but it's more than that. These men are at a whole different level. They're the men we've been expecting all along.

Chi wastes no time in defending us. She quickly sends two discs flying toward them as she takes off. Multiple guns react simultaneously, sending a barrage of bullets at her. Even though she's able to evade the majority of the onslaught, she falls to the ground. Gun downed but still alive.

Holding some sort of plastic weapon, the cronies quickly target each of us. Ava gasps.

I don't even need to guess what's causing her look of horror. I already know. It's Mitchell.

Mitchell, huge and imposing, is standing in the doorway glaring at me.

I know what he's wanted to do to me; he's made it perfectly clear. This time, though, it's different. This time, as I lay here wounded and bleeding, I realize there's nothing to stop him and his rage.

Guida steps forward, drawing his gaze. I don't know what's odder, the way she's staring at him, smiling as if keenly interested, or the way he's looking back at her. Either way, this silent interchange has me wondering if our futures are as irrevocable as I thought just a moment ago. Mitchell, as if questioning his inclination toward my immediate extermination, examines Guida's eyes, then my own. Looking between us, it's as if he's trying to connect the dots. Trying to figure out how this person that came out of the cave could be connected to me, connected to the freak.

Tom breaks Mitchell's moment of reflection.

"Mitchell, I was wondering when you were going to show up," he says, eyeing the guy holding the gun in front of him as if half-expecting to be shot just for talking.

Not one to disappoint, one of the cronies cocks his gun, taking aim at Tom's legs. Even though he doesn't shoot him, it's enough of a threat to make Tom flinch with anticipation. Mitchell, ignoring Tom completely, doesn't say a word. Could he be any more intimidating? I think as I look around the room, purposely not looking at my own legs but feeling the bullet in each of my thighs. Even distracted by the pain, I can't help but feel frighteningly impressed as I observe Mitchell's men. The earlier team having come to their senses, they have positioned themselves among the new team.

One of the men brings something over to Mitchell then. Spotting the bloody gouge in the side of his head, I can only assume its one of Chi's discs.

Mitchell takes it and without even glancing at it says to Tom suddenly, "Tom Perlow. Let me guess. The self-appointed leader of this group of misfits."

Tom bristles as he replies, "Misfits. Sure, whatever you say, you simpleton."

Mitchell arches his eyebrow then gives a slight nod to one of his men. Shots ring out right before Tom yells out and hits the ground.

"You've always been cunning, I'll give you that, but I'd watch that smart mouth of yours when you're in my company," Mitchell says as if not even noticing Tom writhing in agony.

Returning his full attention to the disc, he admires it for a second then pushes the button in the center. The serrated blade instantly retracts into the center. Mitchell seems surprised then chuckles.

"I have to say," he says slowly walking over to Chi as she lies on the ground still and silent, as if willing herself to heal faster. He pushes the button, causing the blades to appear again. "What I saw you do with these was very impressive. Hell, you are very impressive … if it were a different time, different place," he says and smiles smugly right before he violently whips the disc at her. Although lacking her expertise in precision, he's still able to send it cutting through her shoulder.

A small wince is her only reaction before briefly glancing down at the disc then back up at Mitchell. It's written all over her face, and when she smiles up at him, he understands. She's mocking his lack of skill.

He laughs, a hearty, full laugh. Something I've never heard from him. It's disgustingly apparent that he must find her appealing on some level. I shiver as I wonder if anything the monks taught her could have prepared her for this.

"Wireless cameras, of course," Gregor says suddenly staring at the wall by the entrance to the room. Sure enough, stuck up on the wall on either side are two lenses.

"Yeah, big brother was watching," he says and chuckles. "I have to say, even though it was a moronic sight from where I stood, it was informative."

"That's how you knew to use plastic guns. Titanium pins, too, I'm sure," Gregor says putting the pieces together.

"No, I already knew you'd have this place equipped with that scanner technology; hell, one of your people provided me with these guns months ago to puzzle around it."

"Miss Welch."

"Yep, tasty little Miss Welch. What, you thought you and I were the only two-timers working for Irina? No, that woman was so off her rocker at the end. I don't know of anyone who wasn't looking for ways to jump ship. I just didn't realize you had teamed up with the freaks."

"Gregor's always been part of my team," Tom says still dealing with his gunshot wounds but sounding angry regardless.

I watch Mitchell working through it in his mind, getting more pissed by the second as he seems to be understanding the full scope of Gregor's deceit.

"Irina?"

"Already taken care of," Tom says enjoying the disclosure. "Your little redhead too."

"Is that so? Well, that's too bad, I was looking forward to putting them both down myself. Seems as though I'll have to get my satisfaction elsewhere," he says threateningly as he glances at me.

My pulse instantly reacts to the look, even though my pain has finally subsided. I suddenly feel the bullets fall out of the holes in my legs. So this is how we heal from a gunshot wound … the flesh heals from the inside out evicting any foreign object along the way. I'd be much more impressed by it all, if I wasn't still digesting the fact I was shot in the first place.

Ava gasps then looks right at me when she notices the flattened bullets now lying on the floor. Our interchange isn't lost on Mitchell.

"Now I know what you're capable of, little girl. Play nice and I won't hurt you."

"Hey dick, why don't you pick on someone your own size," Tom says protectively as if trying to draw Mitchell's attention away from Ava.

"You're right," Mitchell says eyeing me. "I should pick on someone my size, well … almost my size."

Part of me suddenly realizes what he's talking about, instantly igniting that fire deep within me.

Mitchell sneers at me, and it's then that I know I'm about to see the full scope of his wrath. "He's going to kill Mark to hurt me," I hear myself say to Ava in an anguished loud whisper.

The realization spurs me to finally react just as I sense her movement ... feel the slight pressure on my chest ... Ava's hand. My body moves then, but not of my own accord.

Ava has done what I should have long before now. What took the thought of Mark dying to do ... to finally act.

A look of surprise runs across Mitchell's face when he finds me suddenly standing right in front of him. Rage, deep-seated and honed in on him, quickly comes to the surface. My intent is to kill.

Just as the vision takes hold, I hear something I've never heard before ... Mitchell in pain.

Enveloped in a dull amber glow, each stone that surrounds me is familiar ... trying to connect to that part of me that I don't fully understand ... the part everyone's scared of.

My body, aching and broken, falters.

"Find the darkness ... use it," Mitchell says as he grabs all that is good in me, crushing it with words I so need to hear, words I have to hear. The brutality of his actions has never compared to his words, his reasoning.

The sweet smell of death is all around, filling every crevasse.

Even as the storm begins raging ... it's cruel participation in this war, his presence is the edge I need.

She stares up at me. Scared, sad, but willing ... pleading for me to make the choice.

"I know now why you're the one," he says with the resounding certainty only he could possess. That's when I realize our kinship, our similarities aren't what I need.

No, what I need is his respect.

17

—

Mitchell shoves me away, instantly breaking our connection. I fall back onto the floor, and although I know the world around us has changed, is changing ... we just stare at each other. The man I hate, someone I have wanted dead so many times, now towers over me just as shocked and confused as I am. Another bond forged between us by destiny.

Swinging around, he dismisses what's just taken place between us as he searches the room. Mark runs up and helps me to my feet. He's alive, healthy, and relieved to see me the same way. We both take a mere second to revel in this awareness.

Mitchell stiffens as one of his men triggers something in his eyes. Recognition.

I follow his gaze, expecting the entire place to be in a state of chaos but am surprised to find it just mildly disrupted. Most of Mitchell's cronies have either left or in the process. The whole thing is odd ... their reaction to me branding him.

"You branding Mitchell seemed to mess with their heads," Mark says eyeing a crony standing off to the side seemingly unsure of what to do. "After that, they started leaving."

"Leaving?"

"Little girl, you need to get everyone out of here now," Mitchell says walking right up to Ava. "There's a bomb."

"A bomb," Tom asks glancing down at his legs as he still lies on the ground, bleeding ... healing.

"You see my men leaving. There's a good reason for that."

In the next second, Sandy is there, ignoring Mitchell and Tom's contemptuous interchange as he grabs Ava's arm bringing her over to me. Before I can react, he shoves her hand in my chest.

"Send her!"

I try to pull myself away as I turn toward Mark. Slammed with a sudden reeling sensation, I'm sent away.

Seconds later and I'm standing in Sandy's cabin facing Harrison.

"I can't be here ... I have to..."

I feel panicky, frantic at the thought that I've been banished. No longer there to help protect those I care about.

Without hesitation, Harrison places his finger on the top of my forehead and presses ever so slightly. This simple movement, the feel of his gentle pressure against my skin, instantly calms my mind.

As I'm still reveling in the affect he just had on me, there's movement to my left.

It's Mark. Ava has sent Mark over.

Throwing myself in his arms sends him off balance. "Whoa, everything's still a little loopy," he says, able to keep us both from toppling.

A minute later and Chi is there, healed and standing. Disoriented, she looks around the room until her gaze falls on me. Although probably wondering how she ended up in this place, her one true interest still seems to be keeping me in her line of sight.

Right after Joshua and Gregor, Guida appears. So she isn't immune to Ava's charms after all.

Suddenly Gio appears on the floor, lying in a fetal position, her hair spilling out all around her. Gregor and Harrison immediately run to her.

"She's okay. Let's just move her over there," Gregor says pointing to the brown couch, the same one that I've found refuge. Mark heads over to help.

"The sedation's wearing off," Gregor says as I watch Gio's eyes begin to flutter. Boy is she going to be surprised by everything that's happened, and I have a feeling finding herself here is going to be the least of it.

As if on cue with my thoughts, Mitchell appears. A shiver instantly runs up my spine and I realize this is one man I'm going to have a hard accepting as part of the team.

Tom is next, still healing but at least standing.

Ava—where is she? She can't transport herself. How is she going to make it out? Then I realize Sandy isn't here yet either. Tom's staring at me—he knows I know. His strange look of sympathy turns to anger as soon as he spots him.

"Mitchell, you son of a bitch," Tom says walking up to the huge monster of a man. Mitchell bristles as he crosses his arms and stares down at Tom.

"A bomb ... really. That was your plan?"

Mitchell, not used to having someone in his face, glares at Tom. I can see the muscles in his neck contract. He's having to cage his anger, control his urge to beat the hell out of Tom.

"If I couldn't take you down, I'd at least take you out."

"Well, that's strategy for you," Tom says sarcastically.

For a moment, it looks as though Mitchell may just flatten Tom but then surprisingly he seems to gain control.

"It was a last resort call ... one I never expected to use. Of course, I find when I'm dealing with her, having expectations at all is a mistake," he says glancing my way.

"What's the blast zone ... do they even stand a chance?"

A wave of nausea courses through my body at the thought of anything happening to them. Sandy's always been there for me, for everyone. If there's a hero in this group, it's him. And Ava, so young, so sweet … I should be there to help.

"They'll be fine," I hear Harrison say. "I've seen it."

"What's this kid talking about?" Mitchell asks glancing between Harrison, Gregor, and Mark. He's not slow and it's pretty obvious that they're related. Although Mark's the biggest of the three, their resemblance to each other is undeniable.

"I had another vision," Harrison says to Tom and Gregor.

"You saw Sandy and Ava."

"Yes, I've seen those of us that have been branded standing in that same cave as before, right before the meteorite…"

"What?"

"I don't know, it was weird," Harrison says as if trying to think back to what he saw. "Either way I saw Sandy and Ava, that I'm sure of."

"So you're all on board with him," Mitchell asks.

"This kid has a lot more going for him than you."

Hearing her voice, I spin around. Gio, holding a blanket from the couch around her shoulders, stands there challenging Mitchell with her gaze.

Mitchell smirks. "So, you survived. I have to say, Gregor, I'm impressed."

"I didn't—I mean, Jo branded her," Gregor says as if uncomfortable taking any credit for saving Gio.

"Branded, you mean one of these," Mitchell says exposing his own proof of membership. "I figured this had to have something to do with your little group."

The way he looks at me then tells me our vision was another clue for him.

"You know, I'm still a little surprised you're a part of all this. I mean, you being a dick and all," Tom says so matter-of-factly that Mitchell thinks he's kidding for a second then realizes he not.

"Yeah well, obviously a dick's what you freaks need. What I'd like to know is what exactly I've been signed up to do?"

"I agree. I suppose I'd also appreciate a clearer explanation of our expectations," Gregor says looking to Guida as if this is a conversation that's been a long time coming.

Guida glances around the room like someone about to start a presentation, with the whole dramatic pause and everything, but instead Harrison speaks.

"Your ... our planet has always had humans searching for answers. Most on her planet believe that it was that search for answers that sealed our fate," Harrison says almost relieved to be able to understand Guida.

"How could a search for answers seal our fate?" Gregor asks.

Harrison glances at Guida. "Uh ... a while ago, I guess years ago, someone here discovered that there could be life on others planets."

Gregor seemingly surprised to hear his son's explanation looks between Harrison and Guida. "Yes, the possibility of other habitable planets beyond our own, but what does that have to do with all of this."

"This exploration is what got earth noticed."

"Noticed ... that's incredible."

"Well I don't know," Tom says "I think it kind of depends on who noticed us."

"I know the discovery you're referring to," Gregor says. "It was an incident that occurred years ago, and although undocumented, it took my facet of the scientific community into what I always perceived to be an unorthodox direction."

"What direction?" Mitchell asks as if trying to gather all the information he can before deciding if we really are just a club of wackos.

"We were able to find preliminary evidence of the possibility of life on other worlds." Gregor smiles as if he's a little kid about to tell the biggest secret in the world. "Simple biogenic compounds in meteorites that had fallen to earth."

"That's why he was practically salivating at the thought of getting his hands on that meteorite in the cave," Tom says.

"I was," Gregor says agreeing whole-heartedly. "It could hold the answers to key questions about the ability of extraterrestrial objects or planets to have the appropriate geochemistry to sustain life."

"She doesn't do that for you?" Mitchell asks nodding toward Guida.

Gregor laughs a little. "Of course … that was before."

"This is all very interesting, but I'd still like to know what it has to do with me and this brand," Mitchell says.

"As fate would have it, our humans, uh … astronomers and scientists, I guess," Harrison says, "are about to make an even larger discovery. One that will change our beliefs, or old questions, wait … answer age-old questions, that's it," Harrison says. "It starts with a colliding telescope?"

"The Hubble telescope … and hadron colliders … has to be," Gregor says looking extremely excited.

"Yes …"

"It's unbelievable. These mechanisms are involved with the search for other universes … exoplanets," Gregor says.

"Exo … what?" Tom asks.

"Planets that exhibit earth-like properties, conditions similar to earth. To actually find these planets in the Goldilocks, uh … the habitable zone would be spectacular. Those in astrophysics would be–"

"You know, I think I saw that episode of Star Trek, too," Mitchell says sarcastically as if he's having a hard time taking all this seriously, and I have to agree, this discussion is sounding insane.

Guida looks at me, making me feel like the bad kid in class.

Harrison then goes on to say, "We study our earth in relation to the sun and how it is effected by the other planets in our solar system. Her ... Guida's world is different because of its suns and specific orbiting planets. It's uh, family ... celestial family," he says as if shocked he got it right. "Our scientists are about to consider this difference when attempting to discover other inhabitable planets in other systems. Once they do and begin exploration, discovery is guaranteed."

"My god ... it could definitely be so," Gregor says in shock.

Guida finally speaks, "This is why your world after my own ... is destined to be attacked and destroyed."

Mitchell and Gio are stunned.

"Yeah, takes a little getting used to," Tom says.

"I'm sorry, but are you telling us ... we're going to be destroyed?" Gio asks.

"Yes," Guida says so matter-of-factly that she seems almost resigned to it.

"Well, that's a problem," Mitchell says sarcastically.

"Don't worry, that's not what I've seen. At least I don't think so, I mean ... it's sometimes fuzzy or whatever but ... I don't believe that's our destiny." Harrison says.

Guida stares at him, her eyes not doing their usual movement. No, for the first time, they are still, focused completely on him.

"You speak again of Jo's free will. As you did earlier when I spoke of her destiny with Sandy ... that the two of them shall be one."

Mark looks at me.

All I can do is stare at the floor as my entire body shudders at the thought of how he must be feeling right now.

"Well yeah, of course I believe she has free will . . . " Harrison looks toward Mark.

"That is why your counsel and beliefs guide the prophecy."

"My counsel and beliefs. You mean the destiny, free will thing?"

"Exactly."

"But how can anyone go against destiny?" Mark asks with an edge to his voice like I've never heard before.

"It's done everyday on your world. That's why the prophecy is tied to Jo and the others—to earth. Your kind brings a way of thinking that has long become obsolete on my world."

"You've come here because we think for ourselves," Tom asks.

"I've come here to help guide. If the prophecy comes to be, then the chosen twelve will save my planet ... and yours as well."

"Someone mind telling me what the prophecy actually is," Mitchell says.

Tom fills him in as I watch Mark brood. I feel sick to my stomach knowing how he must be feeling right now. Nothing I can do will change what was said but I would do anything to keep him from feeling the pain of it.

"I've seen enough to buy what your selling but how do we know it'll work? I mean, sounds to me like we're just going off of some kids random visions and her impulses," Mitchell says nodding towards me.

"We should also think in terms of practicality," Gregor adds.

"Practicality?"

"Is the chemical environment even appropriate for us on Guida's planet?" he asks as he begins to pace the room. "And is there an energy source that serves as the geochemical factor for habitability? What about the planet's sun?"

"Suns," Guida says as if enjoying Gregor's unending questions.

"Suns ... yes, of course. That would be most probable. Are the suns the right luminosity to sustain life?"

"Gregor, you're driving me nuts," Tom says.

Gregor nods but can't help himself.

"Tom had said earlier in the warehouse that the meteorite is the portal we will use for traveling to your planet. How is it that only those branded are able to go near it without spontaneously combusting?"

"It has to do with Jo. She's connected to us all ... the one true source. When she brands you it effects your life source, the energy that feeds your abilities."

"So, she's connected to my abilities," Mitchell asks.

"Does that bother you?" Tom asks looking him suspiciously.

"Not nearly as much as learning that it makes me some-how connected to you," Mitchell says dismissively.

Tom bristles. "By the way, I noticed how well you've been taking all this. Hell, wasn't it you that said something about us being a bunch of misfits, and now you're like sign me up."

"What, you don't trust me?"

"Never."

"Good. I wouldn't want to be involved with anyone that did," Mitchell says and seems to come to a decision all of a sudden. "You got good instincts, Tom. You always have, but this time you got it all wrong."

"Do I?" Tom says suspiciously.

"Yes, I plan on being team player with this."

"Really. I find that hard to believe."

"No you don't. You just need confirmation that Jo did more than just mark me. That she connected herself to me in a way that I'm still trying to make sense of. The same way that she probably connected herself to you."

"Not the same way, that I'm sure of," Tom says irritated.

"Either way, I can only assume everyone in this room has been branded. How many in all so far?" Mitchell asks Tom.

"She still has three to choose. Joshua and Mark aren't part of the twelve," Tom answers him as if completely unaware of how it would make Mark feel to hear it.

"Wait a second, I get why the geek wasn't chosen. You always need that person to man the getaway car," Mitchell says then glances toward Mark.

"But you mean to tell me the boyfriend wasn't, or is the other guy the boyfriend now? The model-looking one."

I fume. How can he act like a team player one minute and a complete jerk the next?

"Why don't you shut the hell up?" Mark says coming toward Mitchell all of a sudden.

Mitchell instantly seems delighted at Mark's response. I guess he's just not willing to let his reputation as a bastard go so easily, not even to save the world.

They each hold their ground. The two largest people in the room confronting each other.

"Wait, that's right. You can't be chosen ... being a lower life form and all."

I can tell right away the comment stings. Mark's pissed, and why shouldn't he be? He's had to sit here and listen to a conversation about a life that his father, brother, and girlfriend have that he's not a part of. Plus the whole Sandy thing.

Mark swings, punching him squarely in the jaw. The force of the blow sends Mitchell back a few steps as his head swings to the side. Mitchell seems surprised by the hit then looks at Mark as if he's impressed.

"Obviously you can be an asshole and still become part of the group," Mark says taunting him.

My breath catches as I watch Mitchell smile, blood oozing through his teeth.

My body's on edge. I want to run in and stop this, but what would Mark think if I did?

"Man, I haven't been able to fight old-school in a while," Mitchell says slowly rolling up the sleeves on his shirt.

"You going to keep talking?" Mark says, taunting him still.

"You got a pair, big guy, I'll give you that," Mitchell says then takes a swing at Mark. It misses him completely, but quickly I realize he wanted it to. Mark easily dodges the strike, but as he attempts to hit Mitchell himself, Mitchell steps aside suddenly, then adds to the momentum of the punch to send Mark flying into the wall behind him.

Mark, smashes into the wall, then instantly falls to the ground. I run to him as Mitchell raises his hands.

"I never touched him," he says cockily.

Right as I bend down over Mark, a car pulls up outside. "Mark…"

"I'm fine," he says brushing off my attempts to help him stand.

"It's Sandy and Ava," Tom says from the window.

18

—

S ighing, it's as if I'm able to finally breathe again. Sandy
and Ava are back, safe...

"Holy shit, Sandy, are you even capable of driving
anything that doesn't go from zero to sixty in less than four
seconds?" I hear Tom ask.

"It was parked outside the club. Only one I could get to
at the time," I hear Sandy say as he walks in the door.

"Uh-huh. You know you just stole some punk-ass kid's
reason for living," Tom says chuckling.

Ava runs up to Harrison and surprises him by throwing
her arms around his neck. They both grin, genuinely seem
happy to see each other. The whole exchange is sweet until
Harrison steps back blushing. Glancing my way, I realize why.

Spotting Sandy, I catch him staring at me. He's just as
happy to see me as Ava was to see Harrison but doesn't dare
show it. Not in any affectionate way.

Now that everyone is here, with no injuries and no impending attack, we can all finally take a moment to collect
our thoughts and digest the inevitable.

Tom must be thinking the same. "I don't know about
you guys, but I could use a little R & R. It's late in the morn-
ing and I don't remember the last time I slept or ate anything
that wasn't in bar form," he says headed to the kitchen.

He's right. I know I could use some downtime ... I haven't
had that since the last time I was here. Actually, the cabin's
been the only refuge I've had since this whole thing's started.

I happily welcome what this place represents at the

moment—safety. It may be the only place in my life that ever does.

I turn toward Mark, hoping he's basking in the same feeling of reprieve as the rest of us, but he's gone. He's headed upstairs to Sandy's bedroom. I head up after him knowing this is a conversation we can't avoid.

Maybe he's just tired and is looking to finally get some rest, I think, hopeful but knowing I'm just being a wuss.

I see him as soon as I walk through the door. His back's to me and he's just staring at the wall as I walk in closing the door behind me. I really don't need the whole group to hear our first real fight.

"Mark–"

"Do you love me," he asks without turning around.

"What?"

He looks to the side and I catch sight of his profile. He seems so defeated ... so sad. I know he wants to turn around ... to face me. Probably thinks it's easier on both of us not to.

He asks again, "Do you love me, Jo?"

"Of course."

"Why?" he asks swinging around to face me.

I hear him ask the question, but I don't understand. "Why are you asking me this? You know how I feel about you."

"Exactly. That's why I'm asking. Maybe if you have to say it out loud, maybe then you'll finally realize that it's not love you feel for me. Not the kind you'd have to feel to..."

"To what?"

He turns back around, hiding his face from me. "To sustain..."

I know what he's getting at. It's the same doubts I myself have felt about us. "How could we possibly stay together when everything's always trying to pull us apart?"

He turns around looking at me as if I've just stabbed him in the heart. I realize then I had muttered that last part out loud.

"You're right," he says getting angry now. "How could we be so stupid? To think this could work out."

"I didn't—"

"No, I get it. Besides the fact that you are who you are, I can't compete," he says angrily, a slight quiver to his voice.

"Compete with who?"

"Really, Jo. I mean, my god, aren't you connected in some way to all of those people down there? Actually, I'm pretty sure you have some special connection with everyone except me?"

"But none of that's by choice. I didn't want to brand any of them ... it just happened. I couldn't—"

"It's not just the branding Jo. Hell, even you and my brother are over there talking with each other ... but ... but not talking," he says throwing his hands in the air as he begins to pace.

"Again, it's not my choice ... and he's your younger brother. That's not a connection that you should ever be worried about. In fact, if you want to know how I really feel about you, ask him. He knows all and I mean all of my thoughts."

"Yeah and while I'm at it, why don't I ask him about your feelings for Sandy," he says standing still now, looking at me as if that's one question he wouldn't need to actually ask his brother.

I avoid his gaze as I feel the guilt work its way to the surface.

"That's what I thought," he says so flatly that I glance up. "Don't worry Jo, I'm quite sure those feelings are reciprocated."

I can't argue. How can I? Everyone knows how Sandy

feels about me. But that's not what's bothering Mark though ... no, not Sandy's feelings for me.

A warm, wet tear slowly makes it way down my face as I stand there trying to find the words, a way to tell him that although I love him more than anyone, I do feel something for Sandy. I want to deny it, but I can't.

"I can't lose you," I say knowing I've never said anything more true. "If I lose you..."

My throat tightens as the tears stream down my face.

His look softens right before he grabs me in a tight hug. "I know Jo, and I'm sorry ... sorry for everything," he says his voice cracking.

Why is he sorry? If anyone's ruined things, it's me.

"I mean, I always knew you were meant to do great things ... I just didn't realize those things would take you away from me," he says his voice beginning to break as he holds me tighter.

It dawns on me as I hear his words. I've been so focused on picking the twelve—on my own destiny—that I never realized exactly what I was giving up to fulfill it. I realize it isn't a choice, that trying to save all those lives doesn't make it one ... but that doesn't make it any easier.

I'm stunned as his words sink in. I can feel the barrier I built to keep my thoughts from going to this dark place instantly crumble.

"Jo, you're leaving," he says barely able to get the words out before I feel him breaking in my arms. I'm right there with him.

Opening my eyes, I immediately notice the difference in the sun's brightness. Mark's breathing heavy, steady. He's still in a deep sleep. His arms are still wrapped around me. I ease myself out of them slowly.

We fell asleep holding onto each other, both promising that everything would work out for us. A promise reality may not let us keep.

Leaving the room, I quietly make my way down the stairs, expecting to hear arguing or at least a loud discussion. With Tom and Mitchell under the same roof, I couldn't imagine much else.

Instead everything's strangely quiet. I spot Ava asleep on the large brown couch while Guida sits in the chair next to her just staring up at the large metal circle hanging above the hearth of the fireplace. The twelve symbols etched around the decorative piece draw me in for a moment as I find myself caught up in their familiar embrace.

Guida glances my way, her eyes in full alien mode. Instantly feeling the full weight of my situation again, I give her a slight smile then hurry toward a set of glass doors that lead to the deck, Sandy's own sanctuary from all this craziness. A perfect refuge for someone wanting to find a little peace and quiet. Exactly what I'm looking for at this moment.

Carefully I walk through one of the doors not wanting to disturb Ava. Thinking back on how many people she had to transport in such a small amount of time, I wonder what kind of physical toll it takes on her.

Stepping outside, my senses instantly come alive. My eyes quickly adjust to the new environment. They feel different.

"Jo," Harrison says sitting off to the side on one of the patio chairs. For a moment, I feel as though I may have interrupted him, that maybe he was hoping to be alone also, but he quickly assures me otherwise. "No, I'm glad you're here."

I sit down next to him. "I've really got to get used to being around a mind reader," I say and smile.

"That'd be nice because some of the things you think about, I really don't want to know."

We both laugh realizing how crazy this situation really is.

Attempting a normal conversation I ask, "Where is everyone?"

"Oh, well, after you and Mark went upstairs..."

Think nothing ... think nothing ... think nothing.

He grins at me. "Thanks."

"No problem," I say grinning back.

He continues, "They all left. There was this big discussion about The Order and how they're out of the picture now. How things kind of fell into place even with the bomb blowing up a large portion of the warehouse and all."

"So there really was a bomb?"

"Yeah, I guess so."

"What about Mitchell?"

"Now that he's a part of this whole thing, there's nobody for us to really worry about."

That's going to be hard to get used to.

"That's exactly what Tom said," he says reading my thoughts and smiling.

"I bet he did. So where did everyone go?".

"Some of them had things they wanted to take care of before we leave. So they had Ava transport them different places, to rest, shower, that kind of stuff."

"Oh, well that makes sense," I say realizing how practical it all sounds. Just when I thought it couldn't get weirder.

"Yeah, I know what you mean," he says and a second later we both laugh.

"There wasn't anywhere you wanted to go?" I ask wondering if Ava being here was the reason why he stayed.

The look on his face makes me instantly regret the thought. "Sorry, I … It's just you two are so cute together," I say blurting out the first thing that jumps in my mind.

"Yeah … I got that," he says smiling.

"It's just I think of Ava as my little sister and you're Mark's little brother so it's just too–"

"Cute … yeah, I know," he says still smiling. "I know this is going to sound weird," he says seeming uncomfortable all of a sudden. "But it's just … I've never liked a girl before."

"Oh no, it's not weird at all," I say. "When I was your age, I liked someone for way too long. Now that was weird," I say thinking of all those times I'd sit in the shadows and watch Mark play basketball on his driveway.

I instantly realize the thought and find myself blushing.

"You're right, that is kinda weird," he says grinning now. Then we both burst out laughing, and I realize I can't remember the last time I laughed so much.

My thought sombers him immediately. He glances at me as if he's feeling sorry about something, but what could he be sorry about?

"I'm sorry about everything you've had to go through lately," he says answering me.

I keep my mind blank. I know what he's referring to, but I'm not about to go there right now.

"Jo, I'm not trying to bring it up, it's just … when you remember, when you go to those dark places in your mind … you're not alone. You think that you are, but you're not … I'm with you, and I know that's weird and all, but … it's not just me. I mean, I don't have to read Mark's mind … or even Sandy's"—he says looking straight ahead—"to know how they feel about you."

He hits a nerve, but I'm instantly thankful.

"I guess I just wanted you to know … you really aren't alone in all this."

"I think that a lot, don't I?"

"No, not really. You mostly feel it," he says.

I realize then our connection is more than him reading my thoughts.

"It's a lot more," he says still staring out.

I'm not surprised by his words. I know what he's saying, I don't know how ... I just do. Taking a minute to digest it all, I concentrate on the woods surrounding us. My new super-hearing and hyper-vision have been honing in on everything going on around us this whole time.

Only now as I focus, I notice the slight rustle of the leaves, the scraping of nails against the bark of a tree, all the other noises various small animals have been making. Talk about multitasking.

"You know, like I told Guida, when you were in the cave, when you touched the meteorite for the first time—I saw it," he says obviously wanting to talk about something else and figuring I've had enough time with the woodland creatures.

"So you saw me when I was branded," I say trying not to think back on it.

"Yes, I mean I saw a lot of things ... crazy stuff. All kinds of things but when I saw you it was different."

"Different?" I ask feeling bad, knowing that whatever he went through ... it must have been frightening to go through that alone, without any kind of heads up.

"Yeah, I was pretty freaked out at first," he says. "I was seeing all this crazy stuff and doing everything I could to stop seeing it ... to push the visions out of my head."

"I know the feeling," I say and we smile at each other.

"Once I accepted the fact that all this crazy stuff I was seeing was real, or going to be real, I just started paying attention. That's when it all changed, when I really started to understand everything. It was because I was doing more than paying attention to what I was seeing but started paying attention to how it made me feel. When I had the visions I would get these vibes, feelings or whatever, and well, I know it sounds weird but when I focused on those, that's when everything would become clear."

"Actually, it makes perfect sense."

"So that's how it works with you Jo, it's just ... more. I feel more," he says as if wanting to explain why he's so connected to me. "It's not that I want to invade your private thoughts and feelings ... trust me," he says smiling. "It's just I have no control over it. I just do it."

Another thing we have in common ... our lack of control over our abilities.

He doesn't acknowledge the thought, but I know he heard it.

We just sit there for a few minutes looking out into the woods. Neither one of us says a word as I try and keep my thoughts clear.

We both enjoy this time, this feeling of camaraderie. We enjoy it because we both know that with whatever's coming, Mark's little brother and I have the biggest part to play.

He and I have the biggest part in saving the world.

19

leave Harrison and walk back into the cabin, passing Guida on her way out. I smile to myself when I think about those two having a conversation. Harrison trying to figure out what she's trying to say while the whole time she doesn't utter a word.

I'm glad I had that time with him. I've never really known him as anything other than Mark's brother ... I mean, who would have thought he'd ever be anything to me other than that.

I head for the kitchen. Tom's comment about food last night catches up with me. I'm starving. Walking in, I glance around noticing I wasn't the only one hungry. The counters and tables are cluttered with the remnants of what seems to be an earlier engorgement. Wrappers along with discarded empty bottles and cans are mingled in with a barrage of crumbs, spills, and splattering of condiments across a multitude of dirty dishes left lying around as if the urgency to leave after eating was just as pressing as the hunger itself.

"Yeah, the place is kind of a mess," I hear Sandy say behind me.

Freshly showered with clean clothes on, he's leaning against the door frame smiling. I know part of the whole abilities thing is being easy on the eyes, but sometimes I forget how, even among attractive people, he still stands out.

"You okay?" he asks.

I can feel myself blush, but he doesn't seem to notice. Is

it that he's so used to females staring at him speechless, or does he really not know the effect he has?

"You're hungry," he says misinterpreting my stare but not the growl of my stomach as it tries to remind me why I came in here in the first place.

"I'm afraid I can't make you a sandwich, but I do have a Coke," he says setting the drink in front of me as he searches through what's left of the food in the fridge. I watch him and wonder how my old self would have reacted to having someone like him digging through a refrigerator searching for something, anything just to satisfy me.

He holds up what looks to be an ancient jar of withered pickles and laughs when I start frantically shaking my head.

"I'm afraid they've cleaned me out unless…"

Closing the fridge door, he heads to the pantry and pulls out a box of crackers and a can of tuna.

"How's this?" he asks uncertainly.

"It's fine," I say knowing I've run out of options but wanting to reassure him.

"Don't worry, I won't starve to death before this prophecy even starts," I say smiling at him.

"Yeah, I would hope Harrison would have seen that in one of his visions," he says smiling.

Harrison suddenly comes in as if the weight of the world is on his shoulders.

"Tonight's a lunar eclipse."

"Oh, well, that's cool," I say wondering what that has to do with the worrisome expression on his face.

"No, you don't understand. I've been seeing a red planet in my visions. Just this random red planet here and there. Actually it was one of the first things I saw when you went through your change."

"Guida's planet?"

"That's what I thought. I mean, it made sense so I just

figured it was."

"But it's not," Sandy says trying to figure out what he's getting at.

"No. I haven't been seeing a planet. I've been seeing a moon ... our moon."

"Oh, tonight's lunar eclipse. Are they usually red," I ask realizing I know nothing about them.

"Yes, well no ... that's not the point."

"This lunar eclipse has something to do with the prophecy," Sandy says as if starting to understand what Harrison is getting at.

"Yes. It's when it starts."

"What," I say incredulously. "But I still have three people to brand."

"I know, but Guida agrees. We leave tonight. The night of the lunar eclipse."

"We need to tell Tom ... get the others," I say starting to feel panicky.

"Jo," Sandy says turning me to face him, the burden of a difficult conversation lingering in his expression.

"I don't want you taking this the wrong way or..." he says seemingly struggling over finding the words. "I think you should take this time to talk with Mark ... to say goodbye."

My eyes tear up as he hits that trigger.

"I'm not trying to upset you—that's the last thing I want to do, it's just ... we aren't sure how fast things are going to move once you've branded the last person, and I wouldn't want you and him to not have some sort of ... closure."

"Closure?"

"Yes, well ... maybe closure isn't the right word, but what I mean is ... a real chance to say good-bye. So that you're able to focus on things."

I don't know what to say as I stand here contemplating

his words. I know what he's getting at, but having him say it just seems wrong in some way.

"Jo, he's not trying to be a jerk," Harrison says.

I glance his way, and as soon as I do, I can tell Sandy seems irritated.

"Harrison agrees with you," I say not wanting anything weird between them.

Sandy nods then says, "I know things have gotten strange between us because of the soul mate, destiny thing, but this has nothing to do with my feelings or anything like that. I'm just trying to help you ... that's all this is."

"I know," I say and mean it. It would have been a lot easier for him just to sit back and say nothing, to just wait on the sidelines until Mark's out of the picture and then be there for me when I'm most vulnerable. But Sandy would never do that to me—that's how I know his feelings are real ... pure.

"I understand what you're feeling, believe me I do. You love Mark. When he's with you, you feel whole, complete, as if nothing else matters. Everything you do, everything you want has to do with him, and the thought of not having him in your life is more than unbearable, it's not even conceivable. I get it Jo, trust me."

I avoid his gaze.

"It's just that part of you that wants nothing to do with being chosen—the part that's scared, unsure, and doesn't want to say goodbye to Mark. I know that part of you, I understand it. But I also know the other part, the one that I've been seeing more and more since your change. It feels a sense of responsibility, thrives on it. That's the part of you that knows, truly knows you were destined for something bigger. Jo, this is the part you need to tap into ... especially now."

Knowing what I have to do next, I nod before I begin to lose my composure.

He's there, wrapping his arms around me as I start to sob. "I'm so sorry," he whispers to me as he holds me close. "I would do anything for you not to have to go through this, but I'm here to help you."

"Help me say good-bye to Mark," I say looking up at him knowing he can't actually help me say goodbye, but feeling comforted by the fact that at least he understands.

"I'm sure he'll be more than happy to help you say good-bye to me," Mark says angrily, suddenly standing in the doorway.

Quickly, I push away from Sandy, but the damage is done. No matter how much I try to convince him that what he saw, what he heard, isn't what he thinks, I know that really I'd be lying. Other than Sandy's true motives, what he witnessed is exactly what it was … my plans to move forward with my life without him.

"You know, don't worry about it Jo," Mark says glaring at me now. "There's no need to say good-bye. This will do," he says then storms off.

All I can do is stand there wondering how I'm going to make this better. Sandy's right. Mark is the most important thing—the only thing that truly matters to me. It may not be right, but it's the truth, my truth.

The roar of the engine takes me by surprise. Sandy runs out of the kitchen with Harrison and I following. We get to the opened front door just in time to watch Mark peel away in the same car Sandy and Ava had driven up in earlier.

"You have to go after him," Harrison says frantically to me, and by the look on his face it's more than just a suggestion.

I can feel my body respond as I realize Sandy's right— we have no idea what's going to happen once I brand the last person. I may not have time to find Mark before we're beamed over or whatever? If I lose him now, I may not get the chance to talk to him again, ever.

"Help me, please," I say to Sandy, pleading, hoping that any spark of guilt he may be feeling from the scene in the kitchen might sway him.

He hesitates as I know he's contemplating my safety in all this; he always is. Something in his look changes, and a second later he's instructing me to follow him as he blows out into the garage. Once there he reaches underneath a cabinet to grab something as he tells me to get in.

It's the same car from earlier, the one Sandy usually keeps covered, protected in his garage ... the one Mark was dying to find the key for, the bright yellow sports car. If there's any car that could catch up to Mark, I bet it's this one.

I open the door and awkwardly slide in. The musky smell of oiled leather ignites my senses as I find myself cocooned by the seat's hard protective shell. It feels like a race car.

My eyes are drawn to an exotic-looking emblem displaying the words Alfa Romeo positioned in the center of the leather-wrapped steering wheel.

I hear the garage door start to lift as Sandy gets in. He inserts some small square box into the ignition and revs the engine. For a split second my mind jumps to the feeling I have right before one of those crazy-intense roller coasters takes off. Sitting in the hard, upright seats, I half-expect one of those metal safety contraptions to lower over my torso.

Instead, Sandy gives the engine a quick rev right before he takes off. My fingers instinctively grip the edges of my seat as I feel the effects of the acceleration on my body. Within seconds, we've already turned on the paved two-lane road that winds through the woods.

Grasping the wheel, Sandy shifts the gears seamlessly as we race down the road. I know how fast we're driving. Somewhere in my mind I'm aware of it, but as I sit here inside this car, with its small windows and digital instrument panel lit up in red, I feel as detached to what's going on outside as if I were in a rocket being shot into space.

As we speed down the deserted two-lane road, I anxiously stare straight ahead hoping to fly up on the back of Mark's car any second.

I think back to how angry, how hurt he was. I can't leave things that way, but it seems loving me doesn't bring with it any alternative. At least for Mark, it's the only way it can play out. After all, he's the one that's going to be left behind.

"Shouldn't we have caught up with him by now?" I ask knowing for sure that the car Mark's driving has to be much slower than this one.

"We will," he says glancing over at me right before he floors it. Clenching the edges of my seat, I try not to think about what would happen to us if we got into an accident going this speed. All the special healing in the world wouldn't be able to put our pieces back together again.

I suddenly see a dirt road up ahead like the one that leads up to Sandy's cabin. We fly by it as I ask, "What if he's turned off on another road like that one?"

"The only way out of this area is on this main road. That's one of only two other dirt roads besides mine in this area, both of which only lead to cabins that haven't been occupied for years."

"How do you know?"

"Tom," he says matter-of-factly.

"Oh … of course."

"The other one is two miles up."

"How do you know he didn't turn down the one we passed and go to that cabin? He couldn't know where the road leads."

"He's not that far ahead of us … we'd have seen the dust."

"But what—"

"Hold on," Sandy says tensely just as I see it too—a car up ahead, in the middle of the road, slamming on its brakes. I realize quickly, it's not just any car but the one Mark was driving. As we close in fast, I watch as he stops the car completely, blocking both lanes. He scrambles out of the car just as we fly up on him.

Just as quickly as Sandy's car was able to jet off to incredible speeds, it's able to come to a complete stop in the middle of the road right by Mark's car. My body, still adjusting to a change in momentum, doesn't react as quickly as I want as I attempt to jump out of the car. Mark, now on the opposite side of his car, bends down. What's he doing? Finally feeling more like myself, I run around the car to get to him.

"She was just lying here," Mark stammers to Sandy and I as we run around the car to find a girl lying in the middle of the road. Bright red hair, like the kind created from a bottle, covers her face as she just lies there on her side ... unmoving.

Mark touches her shoulder then gently turns her over on her back. Her arm, completely limp, falls to the road with enough force that I hear her knuckles crack against the asphalt. Mark pulls her hair away from her face, exposing a girl about my age. Full, perfectly shaped pink-tinged lips surrounded by flawless skin. Familiarly flawless.

As Mark checks her pulse, I notice that surprisingly she doesn't have a mark on her, not even a scratch. How could she end up lying in the middle of the road without so much as a scrape?

"She's alive," Mark says looking up at me questioningly as he still bends down over her.

"You're right, I am," she says suddenly opening her eyes and smiling wickedly up at him. He doesn't have time to react before she's up in a flash producing a knife.

I start to respond but then hear the cocking of a gun.

"I'll give you one second to step away from her," a male voice says all of a sudden from behind me.

Turning around, we're face to face with an exact replica of the girl ... just a boy version only with rich dark hair instead of the obnoxiously loud color. Their stances, also similar, display lithe, muscular frames, like swimmers or professional dancers. He's standing at the end of a dirt road. Must be that other one Sandy was talking about that leads to one of the other cabins.

He lowers the gun slightly as he stares at me disbelievingly for a second. I know my eyes are in alien mode right now, I can feel it. What I don't understand is why am I having such a strong reaction to these two? After Mitchell and his militarily-trained, gun-loving buddies, I wouldn't think these two people could instill much fear in us, especially not me.

"Your ears were right, little brother, this car looks fast," the girl says checking out the car Mark was driving.

The guy eyes Sandy's car. "But not as–"

"Fast as the other one," the girl says finishing her brother's sentence.

The girl then smiles at her brother as if she's expecting something to happen. "You got the pack?"

Her brother turns slightly so as to show her some faded worn-out looking backpack resting on his back.

I suddenly feel as though Sandy, Mark and I have found ourselves the victims of a con that these two have carried out before ... many times.

"If you two think you're taking my car you're grossly mistaken," Sandy says with an edge to his voice.

"Well, well, brother, I think that sounds like a challenge," the girl says smiling mischievously at the guy.

He doesn't smile back at her, just stands there pointing that gun at us as if he's been through this a thousand times.

"Should we take him up on it?" the girls asks him as if she's saying much more than what we're hearing. I instantly notice a slight shift in her brother's stance right before he nods.

Suddenly, she tosses the knife up in the air just as I notice the guy throw his gun in the same manner, way above his head. A second later and they are gone—vanished. Another second and they are back, just not as they were before.

The girl appears under the gun catching it with ease, just as Mark all of a sudden finds himself in a much closer proximity to the brother with his arm still raised, having just caught the falling knife.

"What the..." I hear Mark utter under his breath just before the brother punches him, sending Mark flying back to the ground. I should be surprised that this guy was able to deliver such a strong blow, but I'm not. I already know the kind of people we're dealing with—people like us, like Sandy and I.

The girl, having taken advantage of her and her brother's momentary feat, has swiftly pointed the gun so Sandy and I are again in its sights. She looks confident, way more confident than she should be.

Suddenly I'm fighting a similar urge—the urge that has stimulated my already honed senses. I hear the click and react.

I push Sandy away as I turn, avoiding the bullet easily. I barely see the girl's wide-eyed stare through the fog of my intentions. With my left hand gripped tightly around her throat, the violence of my actions is nothing compared to what I do next: shove my right hand onto her chest, causing the expected pain, intense and momentarily unrelenting, to erupt from deep within her.

A minute later when the connection breaks, the guy goes flying back away from me. What the hell? I branded him?

I glance around trying to figure out what exactly just happened when I see the girl lying over on the ground where her brother was standing right before I touched her.

Dazed and trying to catch her breath, she just lays there clutching her chest.

Mark grabs my arm giving me a quick once-ever to check that I'm alright.

"They were branded at the same time," Sandy says coming up to Mark and I as if trying to wrap his head around it too.

"What did you just do to us?" the girl croaks to me as she slowly stands up. Her brother goes to her.

"Why would I brand them?"

"I don't know," Sandy says seeming a little confused himself.

"It was destiny," Mark says looking at me angrily. "You know, the whole prophecy thing."

"Mark–"

All of a sudden, Mark's car starts up. A second later and the three of us are watching as they drive away.

"Shit," Sandy says and runs for his car. I take off toward it, but as he opens the door he raises his hand to stop me.

"It's a two-seater," he says hurriedly.

I look at him like I don't understand.

"Stay here with Mark, Jo. I got this ... trust me. There's a cabin down that road ... just wait for me there."

"I'm not letting you–"

"Jo! Don't you understand, this leaves only one more person to brand. Take this time..."

He glances down. Is he trying to find the words?

When he looks at me again, I realize it's not the words he's having trouble with.

"Make things right with Mark … this may be your only chance," he says then jumps in the car and within a few seconds he's racing down the road … alone.

It's not that I doubt his ability to catch those two; hell, he'll just call Tom and they'll work their usual magic. I just feel like I should help in some way. I mean, I'm the one that just branded two random people we met on the side of the road. Two random supposed thieves.

Turning around I quickly become aware that Mark's already taken off toward the cabin on his own. I realize suddenly that what Sandy was saying probably pissed him off even more. I wonder then how much he heard before taking off.

I follow him down the dirt road toward the cabin. I could take off and be there, right beside him within seconds, but I don't. Like Sandy said, I need to make things right, and running up to him blurting out the first thing that comes to my head doesn't usually work well for me.

As I near the cabin, I watch as he just walks in the front door. It was unlocked, which tells me the twins had probably been staying there on the sly.

When I get to the front door, I hesitate, unsure how I'm going to find his mood. Why shouldn't he feel upset, angry even, about everything? He's the one I'm going to be leaving.

I find a moment of courage and step through the door. I instantly find myself in a cozy one-room cabin. Nicely decorated and seemingly new, but tiny. I didn't realize how small this place was from the outside, but I guess I wasn't paying much attention.

Mark's back is to me as he stands in the bedroom area of the cabin. I blurt out the first thing that pops in my head.

"Mark, I'm so sorry," I say walking up behind him, wanting to wrap my arms around him, hug him as reassurance that no matter what, I still love him—still need him. I don't touch him, just stand behind him savoring the closeness of his large frame in my personal space, fearing this might be the last time.

Tears sting my eyes as I finally start to allow thoughts to seep into those vulnerable places where all my insecurities linger.

I don't know if it was a sniffle, or just small sound that gives him an indication of my emotional state, but he suddenly swings around. Our eyes connect and all his anger, his frustration instantly turns to something else entirely.

That's the moment I know—know that I'm not letting him go. The realization triggers a response deep in the core of my being. I know it, can feel it.

Something with my eyes, maybe the way I look at him, causes him to respond. He lifts me up as I wrap my legs around his waist. Desperation takes hold as we frantically kiss while pulling at each other's clothes. We know what we want and we can't seem to get there fast enough.

Seconds later, our clothes off, he takes me over to the bed. As he hovers over me, I begin to feel the fire stir within me. It's the fire from wanting something more than I thought possible. I want him—all of him.

A sharp pain jars my senses just as I hear him moan. His claim of my body quickly melds into pleasure. It's this feeling, exotic and new, that starts to fade as the fire within me begins to rage. A moment later, it's all-consuming.

Mark, linked to me in ways I've never known, suddenly gasps.

The feeling's familiar, but my disbelief over its possibility keeps me connected ... connected to all the other sensations. I feel what's happening but can't help myself. I don't want to. If it is in fact my choice, then I know it's the only one I have.

I slam my hand against his chest. It's when I hear his pain that I know for sure ... know I've made the choice.

Then our vision starts.

Discover more books at

dburgardbooks.com